Horatio B. Rowney

The Wild Tribes Of India

Horatio B. Rowney

The Wild Tribes Of India

ISBN/EAN: 9783742837523

Manufactured in Europe, USA, Canada, Australia, Japa

Cover: Foto ©Andreas Hilbeck / pixelio.de

Manufactured and distributed by brebook publishing software
(www.brebook.com)

Horatio B. Rowney

The Wild Tribes Of India

THE

WILD TRIBES

OF

INDIA

BY

HORATIO BICKERSTAFFE ROWNEY.

" *Wherein of antres vast and deserts idle,*
Rough quarries, rocks, and hills whose heads touch heaven.
It was my hint to speak; . . . . .
And of the Cannibals that each other eat,
The Anthropophagi, and men whose heads
Do grow beneath their shoulders."—OTHELLO.

LONDON:
THOS. DE LA RUE & CO.

1882

[*The right of Translation and Reproduction is reserved.*]

PRINTED BY
THOMAS DE LA RUE AND CO., BUNHILL ROW,
LONDON.

CONTENTS.

PAGE

INTRODUCTORY REMARKS ix

PART I.

THE INTERNAL TRIBES.

CHAPTER I.

Tribes of the Central Provinces 1

CHAPTER II.

Tribes in Western India 23

CHAPTER III.

Tribes of Rájpootáná and the Indian Desert . . 50

CHAPTER IV.

The Kolarian and other Races in Bengal . . . 59

CHAPTER V.

Tribes of the Madrás Presidency . . . - 95

PART II.

THE FRONTIER TRIBES.

CHAPTER I.

TRIBES ON THE NORTH-WESTERN FRONTIER 117

CHAPTER II.

TRIBES ON THE NORTHERN FRONTIER 127

CHAPTER III.

TRIBES ON THE NORTH-EASTERN FRONTIER 148

CHAPTER IV.

TRIBES ON THE EASTERN FRONTIER 196

PART III.

GENERAL REMARKS 205

THE
WILD TRIBES OF INDIA.

INTRODUCTORY REMARKS.

WITHOUT attaching much importance to the distinctions *Aryan* and *Non-Aryan*, it must be conceded that the population of India may be broadly arranged under two distinct divisions—namely, the *Aboriginal* and the *Immigrant*. Between Kurrachee on one side and Chittagong on the other there are more than a hundred passes through the mountain barriers that invest the country—that is, the Suleiman, the Himalaya, and the Arracan mountains; and these have given various races of invaders admittance into a land famous for its wealth from time anterior to the dawn of legend and chronicle. On the other hand, the sacred books of the country, which are undeniably ancient, are full of the accounts of an indigenous population that existed in it prior to the races of the

Sun and the Moon, and describe minutely the fierce conflicts they waged with the invaders of their hearths and home ; and these accounts have evidently a large substratum of truth in them. The aboriginal tribes, we read, were for the most part vanquished and reduced to serfdom, and formed the servile and impurer castes of the Hindu community, amalgamating either wholly or partially with their conquerors. But there were those who did not submit, who fought and receded till they reached parts of the country where the conquerors did not care to seek for them ; and there is no reason to doubt that the dark wild tribes of the interior hills and jungles of India, who differ so widely from the inhabitants of the plains, are the remnants of the stubborn *Dasyas* that did not yield. The condition of the conquering race is now well known, for it has been largely written upon ; but of the aboriginal tribes who retreated before them the general knowledge is yet very inconsiderable. Every inaccessible jungle, hill-tract, and fen-land of the country is occupied by them ; and they are to be seen there even now almost as isolated by manners, language, and prejudices of race from the population by whom they are surrounded as they were in the past. But they are all more or less shy of strangers, and the unhealthiness and inaccessibility of their retreats scarcely invite inquiry or intrusion. We see many parts of the country marked on the maps as "unexplored" or "thinly inhabited," for the best of all reasons that they are malaria-guarded. The English power is of course nominally dominant everywhere; but, in point of fact, these unexplored and thinly inhabited tracts have been to this day only occasionally penetrated here and there by some eager sportsman or zealous missionary, or by an intrepid official whose presence on the spot was required by some exceptional duty. With some of the tribes the outrages perpetrated by them have made our connexion somewhat more intimate than with others; but the information thus collected regarding them is after all but scanty. As a rule the Government officials everywhere have work enough to absorb all their energies, and the jungle and hill tracts receive merely so much of their attention as is absolutely necessary to repel or guard against the raids emanating therefrom. It is scarcely possible under such circumstances to give any very full account of all the wild tribes in the country. What we propose to

do is simply to note down within a short compass
the little that is actually known at present in regard
to their habits, modes of life, and distinguishing
peculiarities.

The chief abode of the aboriginal races to be
described is the centre of the peninsula—namely, the
Vindhya mountains, which run east and west, from
the Ganges to Guzerat, and the broad forest-tract
extending north and south from the neighbourhood
of Allahabad to the banks of the Godavery; but
they are not necessarily the aborigines of the places
they now occupy. In the *Vedas* the *Dasyas* are spoken
of as having given a great deal of trouble and annoy-
ance to the Brahmans; and they were apparently
pushed into their present homes by successive tides
of invaders operating against them, and often appear
as if they were cut off into small parties in their
flight, portions of the same race being found scattered
in different corners of the country. The main divisions of the *Dasya* race as now seen are: the Gonds,
the Bheels, the Kolis, the Mairs and Meenas, the
Khonds, the Koles, and the Sonthals; but they are
not all one people—at least not at the present day,
whatever they may have been in the past. Some

particular features they do share in common, such as
a common physiognomy, consisting of high cheek-
bones, flat noses, and thick lips, a black colour, similar habits of life, and great sameness of character.
But the dissimilarities existing between them are also
great in several respects, as we shall notice more
especially hereafter; and they themselves do not
admit any consanguinity with each other. Grouping
them according to their obvious affinities, the Gonds
are seen congregating in the Central Provinces, the
Bheels and Kolis in Western India, the Mairs and
Meenás in Rájpootáná, the Koles, Sonthál, and
Dhángurs in Bengal, and the Khonds between Orissá
and Madrás; all occupying the wildest parts of each
province respectively, all content to be called the
" Sons of the Earth " or the " Children of the Forests,"
while the people of the plains pride themselves on
their descent from the Sun and the Moon. The
largest number of aborigines are to be seen in the
Central Provinces, and the next largest in the
Tributary Estates of Bengal; while the most savage
specimens are, perhaps, those located within the limits
of the Madrás and Bombay Presidencies. There are
many smaller communities also scattered all over the

peninsula, in every direction except the extreme
south, each with a distinct name and with some
distinguishing trait peculiar to itself; and on the
frontiers—in the west, north, and east—are tribes of
half-breeds, or of outsiders who have pierced through
and settled, who have for ages passed muster with
the aborigines of the country, though still retaining
marked traces of their foreign origin—Afghán, Mongolian, or Indo-Burmese—in their features and habits.
All these tribes hold themselves distinct and aloof
from the people of the plains, though from a desire
to rise above their natural condition they are gradually engrafting on their own the most popular beliefs
and prejudices of their more civilised neighbours.
They are all fit denizens of the places they occupy—
namely, the hills and forests of their respective provinces, which, left to themselves, would in a short
time be overrun by wild beasts, that multiply in India
with such remarkable fecundity. It is the wild tribes
alone that keep these in check. Without them there
would be no traces of habitation on the hills, no
hopes of clearance and settlement in the jungles. It
is true that many of these tribes live very much like
the wild beasts themselves, but still free—free at least

as those wild beasts are. The hatred of tyranny
which drove their ancestors to their present retreats
survives yet in them, the one redeeming feature
in their character being their utter abhorrence of
thraldom and despotism.

PART I.

THE INTERNAL TRIBES.

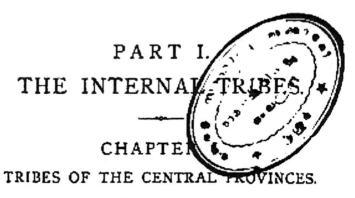

CHAPTER

TRIBES OF THE CENTRAL PROVINCES.

THE GONDS.

THE most numerous of the Indian wild tribes are the
Gonds, who occupy the Central Provinces (or the
very heart of the peninsula), which are divided into
two nearly equal halves by the Sátpoorá hills, that
run south of the Nermuddá river, east and west. The
districts comprised in these Provinces are accordingly
grouped into three classes—namely, those lying north
of, or above, the hills; those belonging to, or em-
braced by, the hills; and those lying south of, or
below, the hills. The districts of the second division
form the hill-region of the entire territory, a great
portion of which belonged to Holkár before the
Mahrattá wars; but at present the plateau of the
hills belongs wholly to the Rájáh of Rewáh, while
the valleys in its neighbourhood are owned by the
British Government. Some parts of the territory are

B

well suited for European settlement, while the rest
are fit only for the habitation of tigers or other wild
animals; and it is here that the Gonds have existed
for ages, and gradually degenerated. A much larger
area was marked out in the older maps of India by
the name of *Gondwana*, or the country of the Gonds,
which seems at one time to have included almost all
the districts both above and below the Sátpoorá
range. The Gonds are understood to have been the
earliest settlers throughout this extent—that is, from
times as far back as history and tradition reach;
while before that period they are supposed to have
occupied places further to the north, whence they
were driven down by successive tides of immigration
from the banks of the Indus. It may at any rate be
taken for granted that they are a very ancient people,
for they are mentioned by name in the *Puránas;* and
it is almost equally certain that they were for a long
period the ruling nation in the provinces in the wilds
of which they now hide themselves.

The first to subjugate the Gonds were the Rájpoots,
with whom the upper ten thousand got mixed in
course of time, whereby they acquired the name of
Ráj Gonds, the traces of whose history can yet be
followed. The unmixed Gonds are known to have
reigned undisturbed in Gurráh up to A.D. 358, and in
Mundlá up to A.D. 634. The throne of the first
state was secured by the Rájpoots by marriage, its
last Gond Rájáh, Nág Deo, being succeeded by his

son-in-law, Jádoo Rái, while Gopál Sháh, the tenth
in succession to Jádoo Rái, acquired the throne of
Mundlá by conquest, and amalgamated it to that of
Gurráh. The four kingdoms finally established by
the Ráj Gonds were Mundlá and Gurráh, Deogurh,
Kherlá, and Chandá, of which the first dominated
over the best part of the Nermuddá Valley, while
the second commanded the heart of the Sátpoorá
range and the southern slopes and plains up to
Nágpore, and the third and fourth the vast wild
territory to the south, down to the banks of the
Godávery. The dynasties that ruled over these
kingdoms were distinct, and they existed up to a
short time before the extinction of the Mogul Empire,
along with a fifth dynasty that was established later
at Wárungul. The Mahomedans had a nominal
control over all these States, and we read how the
Western Gonds, having rebelled against Akbar, were
reduced by him, and how several of the eastern
tribes were converted to Mahomedanism by Au-
rungzebe. But no attempt was ever made by any
of the Emperors to wipe out the nationality of the
Gonds, or to wrest their possessions from them ;
and they did not suffer in that way till after the
Mahomedan Empire was broken up, while the
Mahrattá incursions ebbed and flowed. The severity
with which they were treated during this period
forced them to retire into the hill and jungle recesses they now occupy, while their country became

nominally subject to the Peishwá and other Mahrattá
chiefs—to none of whom, however, were they really
dependent. They rose up in arms against the
English power on Áppa Sáheb of Nágpore seeking
refuge with their Rájáh, Chyn Sháh, in the Mahádeo
hills; and the history of the campaign of 1818 does
speak of some petty reverses sustained there by the
British arms. Eventually, the Gonds and the Mahrattás were both subdued, upon which the mountain
fastnesses of the former were occupied and dismantled, which was succeeded by many efforts made
to cultivate peace and civilisation among them.
There are no traces now of the royal Gond families
of Mundlá and Kherlá; but the descendants of the
princes of Deogurh and Chandá still survive as
pensioners of the State.

The Gonds are a remarkable people, and have
always kept themselves, in the main at least, quite
distinct from all other races. At one time they were
known as reckless robbers and cut-throats; but they
are generally very inoffensive at present, and extremely
shy; and, as a rule, make good cultivators, though
some tribes among them are too lazy for any work
whatever. In the remote past they seem to have
known a more civilised condition, for the *Rig Veda*
speaks of the "cities" and "houses" of the *Dasyus*,
with whom the Gonds may safely be identified; and
remains of Gond architecture of great extent are yet
to be met with in the forests of Mundlá, Deogurh,

Kherlá, and Chandá, including traces of roads, em-
bankments, and irrigation-works, which fill the
traveller with surprise. Their condition now, however, is very low, though of course exceedingly dissimilar in different places. The political changes
they have passed through have divided them into
three classes—namely, the *Assul*, or uncorrupted,
Gonds; the Ráj, or Hindu, Gonds; and the Mahomedan Gonds. According to the localities now
occupied by them, the best known sub-divisions of
the race are the Gurráh Gonds, who inhabit Gurráh,
Mundlá, and Bhopál; the Ráj Gonds, who occupy
Seonee and Deogurh; the Mánjee Gonds, who inhabit
Bustar; the Khullottee Gonds, who occupy the low-
lands east and west of the Lánjee hills; the Jarriá
Gonds, who occupy Chandá; the Máree Gonds, who
live in the wildest parts of the province of Nágpore;
and the Koorkee Gonds, who inhabit the Pachmári
hills. Besides these, there are Gond colonies eastward, in the Cuttack Tributary Mehals, where they
touch the Khonds and the Sours, and westward up
to Kándeish and Málwá, where they touch the Bheels.
The *Assul*, or unmixed, Gonds are to be found most
largely in the unexplored wildernesses between
Chatisgurh and the Godávery, and from the Wyn-
gungá to the eastern Gháts. Their villages are
always situated in the midst of the densest jungles,
and they live the life of wild men there, and have all
the virtues of the wild life in more or less degree,

being especially noted for their straightforwardness
and honesty, and also for their fearlessness in danger,
notwithstanding their extreme shyness of strangers.
The Gonds who live in the open country are, on
the contrary, remarkable only for their meanness,
cowardice, and servility, and have, for the most part,
been brought under the control and domination of the
Hindu population around them.

The personal peculiarities of the entire race are
everywhere nearly the same—namely, a short thick-
set frame, flat nose, thick lips, straight hair, and jet-
black colour, all of which together give to them a
most forbidding appearance. The men shave their
heads, leaving only a top-knot, more or less long,
which yet further disfigures them ; and the women
make themselves hideous by tattooing their faces and
thighs.   Earrings are worn by both sexes, but by the
men on one ear only ; the women decking themselves further with a profusion of bead necklaces of
every colour and size.   At the foot of the mountains,
and in the outskirts of the forests, there is some sort
of dress and an apology for manners, the females
being clad sometimes with leaves, but oftener with a
small cotton cloth wound round their loins ; while
the men pass a yet narrower strip of cloth, the well-
known Indian *kopni*, between their thighs, or have at
places a short *dhoti* to boast of ; but the shades of
barbarism become deeper higher up the mountains
and in the bosom of the woods, where both men and

women—especially among the Mánjee and Máree Gonds—live in a state of nature, with their bodies begrimed with ashes and dirt. Clothing for decency is not understood by these savages, and for warmth they do not mind it, for when the mountain wind is very keen they are content to kindle a roaring fire and sit up around it. If any dressed Gonds appear among them they take alarm and fly, being shy even of their own people when not altogether as barbarous as themselves.

The habits of all the Gonds are uncleanly and degraded, but not equally so in all places. In the gloomier recesses of the forest they live very like the wild beasts around them, subsisting either on roots, berries, and wild honey, eked out by the game they kill with their arrows, or on vermin and reptiles, and these are often to be seen contending with kites and vultures in their eagerness for carrion. Nay, it is said, that in the wilder parts of Chatisgurh, and on the high table-land of Amarkantak, there are tribes yet to be found who cut up and feast on their own relatives and friends when they have become too old or infirm to move about; and it is certain that the Brinjáris, or corn-merchants, who go amongst these people most frequently, never enter the more secluded parts of their country until the gravest protestations of security have been made to them. This, however, is the extreme side of the picture only—not that which is more commonly to be met with. The Gond is

excessively indolent and averse to labour, but his
hills and forests are very productive, and, where he
does labour even a little, he raises with great ease
large supplies of the *kootkee* and *kodon*, which grow
almost spontaneously, and on which he is content to
exist.   The process of cultivation followed is that
called *dhdiyd*, elsewhere known by the name of
jooming, the only instrument used in it being the
hatchet for cutting down trees and brushwood.
When the tract to be cultivated has been cleared,
the cut jungle is set on fire—that is, as soon as it is
dry enough to burn—after which the ashes are distributed on the ground as manure.   The seeds to be
sown are then strewed over the ashes just before the
setting in of the rains ; or, when it is a slope that has
to be cultivated, they are placed at its upper end, it
being left to the rains to wash them down into the
ground prepared for them.   There is no ploughing or
other operation of any kind after this, the crop being
left to come up of itself.   When it has grown, as it
always does in abundance, it is protected with great
care against the depredations of the deer and wild
hog ; and the out-turn thus obtained makes the Gond
almost altogether independent of extraneous assistance.   In those places where a taste for better kinds
of food than the *kootkee* and *kodon* has been acquired,
the Gonds depend mainly on the Brinjáris for their
supply, receiving from them sugar and salt also, which
they have commenced of late to appreciate.   The

only Gonds who have yet learnt to cultivate by ploughing are those who have had Hindu zemindárs over them, and these are able to raise for themselves various crops of wheat, rice, *jhow, urhur, chanud,* maize, *janerá,* oil-seeds, and tobacco. As a rule the western parts of Gondwáná are more fertile and better watered than the rest, and the progress of civilisation there has accordingly been the greatest. The eastern parts of the country lying nearest to the confines of the Cuttack Tributary Estates have also commenced to improve, and an assimilation with Ooryah manners promises in a short time to convert the tribes there located into nearly the same condition with their neighbours.

The tribal divisions among the Gonds are in reality very numerous; but they themselves count twelve-and-a-half tribes only—namely, the Ráj Gonds, Raghuwals, Dadávies, Katulyás, Dholis, Ojhyáls, Thotyáls, Koilálhutuls, Koikopáls, Koláms, Mudyáls, Pádals, and a half-tribe of inferior grade that goes by the same name as the last. The language peculiar to all the septs is the same, and is called *Gondi,* which is spoken throughout their country. There is one tribe called Gours, who, living nearest to the Cuttack frontier, have by some writers been counted along with the Ooryáh tribes. But they are scarcely distinguishable from the Gond races in appearance, disposition, and character, and have blood-relations among them, both to their south and west; besides which it may be noted that the name of "Gour," given to them by the Ooryábs, is only another way of writing and pronouncing the word *Gond*, which, correctly written, ought to be spelt *Gour*.

The Gonds are the most powerful of all the wild tribes in India, at least in numbers, as they count more than a million-and-a-half persons among them, all muscular in development, as we have described them, but sadly deficient in intelligence. The *Assul* Gonds, we have said, live in the densest jungles to this day, and almost entirely by themselves; and even the domestic Gonds can hardly be held to congregate. In the depths of the forests the Gond villages seldom count more than five or six huts each, containing in all some fifteen or twenty inhabitants; while very often there is no more than a single hut to be seen within an area of one or two miles, with a sole Gond for its occupant, and a pig or two for his companions. Even in the open country the largest village has never so many as fifty houses, rarely more than thirty or thirty-five, each hut counting from five to eight souls. The buildings are all of the most miserable kind, with walls built of stakes cut from the nearest jungle entwined with rude wicker-work and plastered over with mud, while the roof consists of a thin layer or coating of dried grass, over which are spread some *praus* leaves, and a few battens made of bamboo fastened over all, to prevent the leaves from being blown off by the wind. Inside the conveniences are yet more slender. Of house-furniture there is none at all, beyond some dry gourds kept for bringing water; no bedding to sleep upon, nor platter to eat from, the leaves of the forest serving all such purposes alike. Even the room available to the inmates is exceedingly scanty, so much so that the bachelors of a village have to live apart by themselves, which is a rather common rule among the wild tribes of India generally, and has probably been adopted with a view to keep the sexes apart, though a perfect separation of them is nowhere attempted to be enforced.

Where the seclusion of life is very great, the chief occupation of the Gond still is to rove about his forests, hatchet in hand, almost without any object to secure, but ready at all times to cut down the trees that obstruct his path, or to contend with the wild beasts that go prowling about him. At one time this life was perhaps more congenial to him than now, and more productive also—that is, when he lived by way-laying travellers and plundering them. The country he dwells in is so difficult and pathless as to be full of nooks and corners which no body of troops—Hindu, Mahomedan, or European—has ever been able to penetrate, and there is no unlikelihood there-fore in the stories related that the travellers met with in these wilds used frequently to be attacked and killed. In the neighbourhood of Amarkantak especially there was, it is said, a favourite mode of

destroying them—namely, by carrying them to the
shrines there to offer their devotions, and then cutting
them down the moment they had prostrated themselves; and during the earlier years of the British
rule in India large numbers of the Gonds were
frequently met with going about the open country
with no other object than the commission of robberies
on a wholesale scale. It has of course become less
possible to indulge in such propensities at present,
which has contributed not a little to make even the
uncorrupted Gonds better behaved and more amenable
to authority now than they ever were. But where
the opportunity of misbehaving arises the will to be
mischievous is never wanting among them; nor are
they ever unprepared for such occasions. The arms
usually carried by the Gonds are the primitive Hindu
weapons, the hatchet, the knife, and the bow and
arrows, all of which they wield with equal dexterity.
The Mahrattás taught them the use of the matchlock
also, when employing them against their enemies; but
they have not many of these weapons with them now.

Among the less wild tribes the general occupation
at present is breeding swine and buffaloes, and
rearing fowls; and it is said of the *Assn!* Gonds that
even the fowls reared by them are as wild as themselves. Many Gonds also take employment now as
coolies, and have been found able and willing to work
at timber-cutting, mining, road-making, and other
tasks of similar character. They are assiduous too

in collecting fuel, lac, unwrought iron, and whatever else is to be found in their hills and forests. They are not less opposed to labour now than before; but the Brinjáris have succeeded in creating new wants and tastes among them, and the price of the supplies they bring in has to be paid. The *soondi*, or spirit-manufacturer, has also introduced distillery-made spirit into their villages, which likewise has to be purchased; and these two causes together have forced them to be more industrious in utilising the produce of their forests than they were accustomed to be before. It has alienated them at the same time from their sanguinary propensities and habits. Before a relish for salt, sugar, and distillery-made spirit was acquired, the Gond was scarcely approachable; but he cannot do without them now, and that has done more to bring him into order than almost anything else. The influence of the Government has been mainly confined to the suppression of open acts of violence, such as murder and dacoity; the tastes created by the *soondis* and the Brinjáris, and the supplies brought in by them, have contributed yet more towards the establishment of general security all over the country, by rendering the presence of strangers in it a necessity to the savages. This has dissipated their reserve to a great extent, and rendered it possible for the *bunniah*, the blacksmith, the carpenter, and the weaver to enter their villages in the wake of the Brinjáris and the *soondis*. All the civilisation.

in fact, that has penetrated those places has been forced into them by the *soondi*, or the Brinjári, or the zemindár, to which three the Gonds owe more for their improvement than to any Government they have ever lived under. The degradation of their actual condition can indeed hardly be more forcibly described than by the perfectly veracious statement that even the conspicuous presence of the *soondi* amongst them at this moment is not an unmitigated evil. The Government has of course very zealously come forward to remedy this state of things by an offer of that panacea for all misfortunes, the Catechism; but the ignorance of the race is profound, and the schools opened for educating them have nowhere been yet largely availed of.

The religion of the Gonds differs materially among the different classes or tribes we have named; but all the unmixed Gonds worship a common deity, differently called Burrá Deo, Bodá Deo, Báum Deo, or Bodeel Peer, who is generally understood to be a representation of the Sun, to whom human sacrifices used to be offered in the past, the substitute for which now is the image of a man made with straw or other similar materials. Among the other deities venerated are representations of the Moon and Stars; but there are no temples for any of them, all the places of worship being in the open air, and simply enclosed by circular walls of loose stone, while the objects worshipped are represented by some two or

three large stones stuck upright and smeared with oil
and *sindoor* or vermilion. The name of Bhaváni is
also respected, as likewise is the tiger, which is considered to be her *báhun*, or riding-animal. The Gonds
thread the jungle-paths at dead of night without the
slightest dread of the tiger; but they seldom attack
it except when it commits great havoc among their
cattle. The belief in supernatural agents, too, is wide-
spread amongst them, and so is the fear of witchcraft
and of the evil eye; and there is nothing they will
not do to guard themselves against these influences.

Of the more remarkable customs among them
those relating to marriage and death have some
peculiarities in them that may here be cursorily referred to. As said before, the separation of the sexes
is provided for by them, but is never very rigidly
enforced. The youths of both sexes, though they
are not allowed to sleep under the same roof at
night, have every facility given to them to meet with
and make love to each other at all hours, though
the final marriage-arrangements always require the
sanction of their parents. The process followed
after this sanction has been secured is for the bridegroom to go forth with his friends to fetch his bride
home, when she affects to be averse to the union, or
not to like a married life at all, and hides herself.
This leads to her being sought for, and, on being
found, which she always manages should be the case,
she is borne off in triumph, after which a great feast

is given by the bridegroom's father to celebrate the event, a cow being killed, and a large supply of *hndi* (the favourite drink of the race), provided for. The cow is eaten by all the *Asrul* and the Mahomedan Gonds, but not by the Ráj Gonds, though it is doubtful if the latter stop short of any animal besides the cow. Over the dead, also, the wild Gonds hold a "wake," all the friends of the deceased being summoned to a mourning-feast, which is in every respect very similar to that given on marriage occasions, and, like it, terminates invariably in excess. As a rule the dead are buried, cremation being performed in especial cases only, when the ashes are interred on the roadside.

The diet of the Gonds is, we have stated, comparatively poor, and excessively filthy; and they have had at all times an inveterate taste for drink, which the introduction of the distillery system in their country has yet further aggravated. They are also great smokers, and he that has no clothing on his body has still a girdle of *cowries* or cords around his waist to suspend therefrom a tobacco-pouch alongside of a naked knife. And yet, notwithstanding such deleterious habits, they are found in all places to be long-lived, and do not soon exhibit signs of old age, retaining sound teeth and black hair almost to the day of their death. Improved food and improved clothing, improved habitations and improved hygiene, are of course as desirable for them as for every other race similarly circumstanced; but they have thriven so well without them hitherto, that the more pressing requirements in their case seem rather to be the introduction of better habits of usefulness and a better appreciation of sustained labour by finding suitable work for them in the midst of their own wildernesses, which they will not abandon for the very best advantages. They are very deficient in intelligence also, but, as they are tractable and obedient under kind treatment, there ought to be no insuperable impediment in the way of improving them even in this respect. They are among the best behaved of the wild tribes now, whatever they may have been before, and on that account, if for nothing else, deserve that everything that can be done for them should be done.

MINOR TRIBES OF THE CENTRAL PROVINCES.

The wild tribes in the Central Provinces include a sprinkling of Kolis and Bheels; but, as these are more powerfully located elsewhere, we shall not allude to them in this place. There are also a great many minor tribes in the country—too many in fact for all of them to be even named by us; but out of them the Brinjáris, already referred to, the Bhowris, or Hareen Shikáris, the Táreemooks, or wandering blacksmiths, the Koráwars, the Bhátoos, and the Mudikpors, may be enumerated.

c

THE BRINJÁRIS.

The Brinjáris are wandering traders, who derive their name from their occupation, and are of various tribes. They were called into existence by the necessities of the Hindu and Mahomedan sovereigns, who wanted expert purveyors for their armies, having never had any commissariat department attached to them ; and no great body of men could move about the country formerly without being accompanied by these itinerant grainsellers, who were well protected by all. Their original occupation is now gone ; but they still go about as before, always in large troops, and accompanied by their families, dogs, and laden bullocks, passing from village to village to supply the wants of the inhabitants, who are all more or less dependent on these visits, even for the very necessaries of life. They are molested by none, though there is hardly any part of India which they do not go to ; but in some places they are compelled to pay some trifling duties for the protection extended to them. It is scarcely correct to say that they belong to the Central Provinces in particular, or to any other part of India, for they come and go from place to place without forming any permanent attachments anywhere. They are most frequently seen in Central India, because their services are in particular demand there, on account of the indolence of the Gonds, whom they supply with food-grains purchased from the

zemindárs, and more especially with salt, sugar, and
other luxuries, receiving in exchange the productions
of their wilds, which they carry to more profitable
markets. They pursue their course through roads
which nothing but the most indefatigable spirit of
industry could induce anyone to attempt, and through
narrow defiles often barely affording passage to them
and their bullocks. The men are tall and well
formed, dressing very like the communities among
whom they move, and having similar manners to a
great extent. Born in the open field, and bred up as
itinerants, they brave the heat of a vertical sun, the
bleak blasts of winter, and the deluges of the rainy
season with equal indifference, and in so doing
acquire a robust constitution which is shared by
their women. They live mostly under tents, except
during the rains, when they set up temporary grass-
huts wherever they may be stopping at the time.
Though nearly as rude as most of the tribes they mix
with, they acquire by necessity some acquaintance
with the arts of life, and are also more industrious
than all of them ; but they are poorer now than they
were before, and with their poverty have become
more criminal too—robbers, cattle-lifters, and Thugs
having been found among them.

THE BHOWRIS.

The Bhowris are also a vagabond race, of shorter
stature than the Brinjáris, and unlike them in this,

C 2

too, that they are very shy and unintelligent, almost
equally so with the Gonds. They, too, are to be seen
in all parts of India, like the Brinjáris, and figure
similarly as thieves on a large scale, though gang-
robbery and offences attended with violence are out
of their line. They hunt wild animals of all kinds,
and eat whatever they kill. Their manners are very
rude; they have hardly any dress at all—nothing in
fact beyond a narrow loin-cloth; and the women are
no better clad than the men. They are nevertheless
very thrifty; and professional dacoits are always on
the look-out for them.

THE TÁREEMOOKS.

The Táreemooks, on the contrary, are a poor and
improvident race, living from hand to mouth. They
are of a dark colour, though not quite so dark as the
Gonds and some of the other tribes, and are a little
taller and better formed than all of them. They are
very laborious also, and are always loyally assisted in
their labours by their women, who collect wood in the
jungles to make charcoal for them, and work their
forge-bellows; but they cannot, for all that, make the
two ends meet, principally from being much addicted
to drink. The life of the tribe, moreover, is very
loose; there is no such thing as constancy among the
men or chastity among the women; and married
men makelove to each other's wives almost openly,
without fear or shame.

THE KORÁWARS.

The Koráwars are of shorter stature, but are otherwise as robustly made as the Táreemooks, having well-knit muscular frames and a large share of energy. They are divided into many sects, some of whom are nomadic and constantly roving, while others lead a settled life. They cultivate a little for themselves, and also make grass-screens and baskets; but they always have more money than can ever be earned by such occupations, and the inference is that they live mainly as dacoits. Their private morals too are very low, and many among them make money by prostituting their women, who are trained up as dancing girls, and attached to the temples as *deh-muttees*, or mistresses of the gods. These women bear children, but that entails no disgrace either on them or on their progeny.

THE BHÁTOOS.

The Bhátoos are a short-sized but well-formed and active race, trained to agile feats from their youth. The exhibition of these feats is their ostensible means of living, and they wander from village to village displaying their nimbleness with the aid of a bamboo, which is worshipped as a god. They call themselves Mahrattás, but the genuine Mahrattás do not acknowledge any relationship with them.

THE MUDIKPORS.

The Mudikpors are tall powerful men, having olive-yellow complexions, and are fishermen by trade, while their women earn a little by knitting and tattooing. They bear the best character of all the minor tribes named, and their females are especially spoken of as being equally honest and assiduous.

CHAPTER II.

TRIBES IN WESTERN INDIA.

THE BHEELS.

THE Bheels are numerically inferior to the Gonds, but are in all other respects a more important race. Their country is called *Bheelwárá*, and embraces the rocky ranges of the Vindhyá, Sátpoorá, and Sát-málli mountains, of which the passes were long held by them; and the jungles on both banks of the Nermuddá, the Táptee, and the Máhee. Popular tradition ascribes to them a fabulous origin from Mahádeva, who is said to have fallen in love with a forest girl, by whom he had a numerous progeny, one of the children being particularly ugly and vicious, who distinguished himself finally by slaying his father's favourite *brisa*, or bull, for which he was expelled from the habitations of men. The Bheels pretend to be descended from this outcast, and to have inherited crime and outlawry as "Mahádeva's thieves"— that is, with their descent. They are divided into so many tribes that the opinion has been hazarded that the name "Bheel," when it was originally assumed, perhaps only denoted a confederacy of various robber-races thrown together and associated by local circumstances and events; but the inference is far-fetched and scarcely tenable, for the Bheels are mentioned as an aboriginal people in the *Mahábhárata*, and the history of India shows that, like the Gonds, they were at one time a ruling race, though not exactly in the places they now occupy. Their original residence, it is supposed, was Márwár or Jodhpore, whence they were driven south by other races; and the local history of the Rájpoot princes confirms the belief by stating that the Bheels were expelled from the plain country by the Rájpoots. Their present quarters were apparently sought for by them in preference to subjection and civilisation when the tides of immigration and conquest were running too strong to be breasted, and, becoming masters of the mountain-passes to which they had retreated, they felt that they were unconquerable, and retained for good the positions they had occupied. The hill tracts of Kándeish and Málwá have thus belonged to them from very remote times; and, as none of the native Governments were ever powerful enough to restrain their lawlessness effectually, their depredations on the rich lowlanders in their immediate vicinity were early commenced and persistently continued. They regarded it, in fact, as their privilege to rob, and, besides always oppressing their neighbours, took advantage of every change in the administration and

every internal commotion to sally forth to greater
distances in quest of victims. Their demands for
black mail were openly made, and many of them
were conveyed in writing, the scraps being left
dangling round the neck of some village idol, or
from some well-known tree, before the village was
attacked. One of these notes has been thus trans-
lated :—

> "From Mohnn Niik
> "To Bholá, Pátel of Keeprá Kairá,
>
> "The moment you receive this note you must bring Rs. 500, which
> are due to us. If any delay occurs we will put your people to death,
> cut off their ears and noses, and help ourselves. Let this be well
> considered."

And the threats thus held out were invariably carried
into effect. All that the administrators of the country
were able to do in return was to entice the robbers
into their power by deceit and stratagem, and those
who fell into the snare were generally very sum-
marily dealt with. During the period of Mahrattá
rule especially the Bheels were entrapped in large
numbers under hopes of pardon and preferment, and
then massacred without remorse. They were viewed
simply as pests and outcasts of society, to exterminate
whom any artifice was held to be justifiable; but
nothing that could be done in that way was ever
able to check their depredations, and their turbulence
had full play down to the falling off of the Mahomedan power. In fact, at this period the Bheels

seem to have advanced more than ever in political strength and status, the struggles between the Mahomedans and the Mahrattas, and the subsequent misgovernment of the Peishwa's officers, having given them the opportunity to start organised bands of dacoits in every direction, headed by Naiks, or chiefs, who assumed all the state of petty princes, and desolated every village or hamlet that was accessible to them. This state of disorder was prolonged till the establishment of the English rule in India, when, the plundering habits of the Bheels bringing them into conflict with that power, Kandeish and Malwa were occupied by Sir John Malcolm in 1818, during the great Mahratta and Pindari war, whereby the political authority of the caterans was terminated.

The first measures taken by the British Government to subdue the Bheels were to stop the supplies of food drawn by them from the plains, and simultaneously to cut off all parties attempting to issue from the hills for purposes of plunder. These steps proving unsuccessful, recourse was had to military operations; and in the struggles that followed many chiefs were killed, while those who were captured were imprisoned, or transported, or hanged. The power of the British arms was now felt to be irresistible; but the Bheels did not yet betray any wish to give in, and fresh chiefs started up to replace those who had been taken and punished. This forced on the Government the adoption of milder measures.

which were commenced by the offer of a general amnesty to all who would submit, with the exception of the most heinous offenders. "You have lived in the hills and plundered the roads and the country," said the proclamation that was issued; "the *Sirkár* has pardoned your past crimes, and you may remain in your villages if you will cultivate the lands and gain your livelihood honestly." With a free pardon were also offered lands, clothes, money, and food; and that many still held out was owing only to their dread of such deceit as had been frequently practised on them before by the native Governments, which always destroyed those whom they were able to entrap. When they found, however, that their fears were groundless, they began to come in in large numbers, and to settle down quietly in different places as *pátels*, or cultivators of the soil; upon which they were furnished with food and the implements of husbandry to learn the new life that was opened out to them, while the possession of their lands was secured to them, with freedom from taxation for a number of years, to make it worth their while to acquire industrious habits. This led to the establishment of the Bheel Agency in 1825, to watch over the colonies that were formed, military operations being thenceforth confined to the pursuit of the armed bands that still infested the wilder parts of the country, which gave almost as much trouble as they experienced themselves, the utmost efforts of the

harnessed soldier being often quite powerless to cope
with them on equal terms. The last reformatory
measure adopted, therefore, was the organisation of
a military corps, which all the unruly Bheels were
invited to enter, and which necessarily contributed
most of all to the eventual pacification of the country.
All classes of Bheels now began to submit in large
numbers, though not without occasional protests
against restraint and subjection to law; and the
habits of the entire nation were thus gradually
changed. The corps did particular service in putting
down the plundering proclivities of their countrymen,
whereby the reforms introduced by the Agency were
allowed time to operate on their character, and to
refashion it. One officer, in writing of the people in
1855, says that, " Instead of living chiefly on plunder,
as we found them doing, it is seldom that any of
them are guilty even of petty gang robbery." This
was an official picture, and over-coloured to a considerable extent; but within the last sixty years the
bulk of a people who were found utterly savage to
commence with have, at least apparently, become reconciled to the peaceful and industrious life that was
chalked out for them. In Kándeish the Bheels form
about one-eighth of the population, and are among
the best behaved and most useful. A great many of
them are wholly devoted to agriculture, and, though
it cannot be said that they have become very successful and prosperous farmers, still in most places

they have become apt to this extent, that they are
not easily distinguishable from the other cultivating
classes around them. Many of them, also, make their
living by the manufacture of baskets, in which they are
very skilful; others collect gums, wax, and honey, and
barter them for the produce of the surrounding countries; others cut and sell firewood and timber, and
all the fruits, roots, and herbs of the jungles; others
take service as ploughmen and day-labourers on the
plains; others kill wild animals for the sake of the
rewards given for them; while others are serving as
soldiers in the Bheel corps, which is distributed over
the province in numerous detachments, and mainly
employed on police duties. Similarly, the Bheels of
Guzerát, who are settled about the banks of the
Máhee, are now engaged almost exclusively in agriculture; while those of Indore, in Hoikár's dominions,
who were at one time among the most wild and
savage, have been largely converted into useful and
trustworthy soldiers, and are fast acquiring agricultural habits also.

The physical characteristics of the Bheels are : a
dark colour, diminutive size, prominent cheek-bones,
large nostrils, and great personal activity combined
with an astonishing power of enduring fatigue. They
are not so long-lived as the Gonds, and become old
at sixty, at which age a Gond usually shows no signs
of decay; but they have more hardihood and agility
than the Gonds, though less of muscular strength

and are so restless by disposition that nothing is
able to reconcile them to purely sedentary pursuits.
The main divisions of the race are known as the
village, the cultivating, and the wild or mountain
Bheels; of whom the first comprise all those who,
from chance or ancient residence, have become inhabitants of the villages of the plains in the immediate
neighbourhood of the hills; the second, all those
who have continued in their peaceable occupations
ever since their gangs were broken up and their
leaders destroyed or driven abroad; and the third,
those who, preferring savage freedom to a life of
comparative comfort under control, live almost as
wild now as before, in the wildest parts of their
mountain country. Of these classes the second and
the third have alternately increased or decreased in
numbers according to the fluctuations of the neighbouring Governments, and are essentially the same
to this day in almost every respect. When the Governments were strong, the cultivating Bheels always
drew recruits from the ranks of their wilder brethren;
while, when the Governments were weak or oppressive,
the industrious Bheels were driven by their behaviour
to join the robber-tribes and adopt their profession
for the time. The village Bheels, on the contrary,
have for a long period lived quite apart from both
the other classes, holding as little intercourse with
them as men of the same race, living in the same
manner generally, and almost side by side with each

other, could possibly manage. Distinguished locally, the chief tribes now residing within British territory are: the Naháls, the Nirdhis, the Khoteels, and the Dáungchees, who still live apart from all others in their mountains and jungles; and the Turvees, the Mutwárees, the Burdás, the Dorepies, the Mowchees, the Parvees, the Wulvees, the Wusáwás, the Wurálás, and the Powerás, most of whom have long subsided into peaceful inhabitants under the fostering care of a benevolent Government. The Naháls inhabit the north-east part of Kándeish, from Arráwád to Boorhánpore, and have a name for untameableness to this day, together with all the wild habits with which their ancestors were credited, living on wild fruits and roots mainly, and on the game obtained by their archery. The character of the Nirdhis, who live about the Ajuntá range, is very similar, and includes a thorough contempt and dislike of labour as it is understood by the more civilised tribes. The Khoteels are the wild inhabitants of the Sátpoorá hills, who, however, collect gums and wax with great patience, and barter them for the produce of the plains. The Dáungchees are the natives of the Dáung below the Western Ghats, and have the reputation of being the most degraded, the most stupid, and the most uncivilised of all the tribes. Of the other clans the Turvees are the neighbours of the Naháls, and live between Arráwád and Boorhánpore, where they are best known at present for their devotion to agri-

culture, though they bore a more disorderly character
during the Pindári times; the Mutwárees, Bunkás,
and Dorepies inhabit the mountain ranges to the
north-west of Kándeish about Akránee and Dher-
gong, and are famed for their skill in basket-making,
besides being good cultivators also; while the Mowchees, Parvees, Wulvees, Wusáwás, Wurálás, and
Powerás, who inhabit the western districts of Sultán-
pore, Tikree, etc., are particularly distinguished for
their pastoral habits, and some of them, such as the
Wurálás, also for rearing domestic fowls in great
abundance.   There are some Bheel tribes besides in
Áhmedábád and Rewáh Kantá, who are named
Bariá, Karit, Pággi, Kotwál, and Naikrá; and many
among these are adepts in cattle-lifting and thieving,
though they have yet more generally betaken to
agriculture at the present day.

All the Bheel tribes do not resemble each other:
for, while the Dáungchees, for instance, are of the
darkest colour and have a forbidding appearance, the
Turvees have a fairer skin and finer features, the
difference between them in other respects being
equally remarkable.   But the reason for this is not
far to find.   The Mogul policy located Mahomedan
colonists among the Bheels, in the hope of keeping
them in check, and perhaps of civilising them.   But
the colonists fraternised with the people they were
appointed to watch over, and got mixed with them,
the only service they did to their Government being

confined to the conversion of many Bheel tribes to
Mahomedanism. The Turvees are believed to be
the descendants of these colonists, while the Dáungchees represent the unadulterated race; both equally
illiterate, but one quick and intelligent, the other
having intellect barely enough to understand the
simplest communications, and totally unequal to com-
prehend anything beyond them. In some cases the
differences between the tribes are so great that it is
often impossible to find any common ground of
affinity between them. But this upon inquiry is
invariably found to be the sequence of gradual
reclamation only.

The country of the Bheels is still as wild as ever;
but a great portion of the population, we have seen,
has now been thoroughly tamed, and accustomed to
industry and labour. The tribes are distinct in some
respects, which we have partially noticed, and, while
some are Hindus, others are Mahomedans, a few
again being neither one nor the other. Even the
languages spoken by them severally are not the same,
at least in all places. But still are they one people,
living almost on the same diet, having the same
usages generally, and bearing the same character
slightly diversified under the distinctions of " wild "
and " reformed," by which they are mainly distinguished. The particulars to be noticed of them are
necessarily in a great measure identical. They are
all wholly illiterate, and some so ignorant that they

D

cannot count, and have no terms to express numbers
beyond twenty; and the schools which have been
opened for them by the Government have nowhere
been much availed of. But they have expression in
their eyes and features, and, though unable to read
and write, have an intelligence which develops with
their condition. In the mountains the wild Bheels
still remain in a state of nature; but the bulk of
those who inhabit the valleys have always a belt of
coarse cloth round their loins, in which they also
carry their knives, and some wrap a second piece of
cloth besides round their heads and shoulders. The
women are even more decently clad than the men,
and are less dirty than the women of the Gonds;
and it is said that they are permitted to assert their
rights pretty freely over their husbands. The beard
and hair of the men used to be kept thick and
dishevelled before, which gave them a wild appearance, and this was very much heightened when they
went armed; but at present the men shave their
faces, and seldom exhibit anything more than a slight
moustache, and, far from being dreaded, they are
themselves getting distrustful and timid. The arms
of the Bheels are the same with those of the Gonds—
namely, the axe, the knife, and the bow and arrows,
the latter two made of the bamboo, the arrows being
tipped with iron heads; and they are all excellent
woodmen and ready hunters to this day. They are
good workmen also, if their patience be not too

severely taxed, and they build their own huts and
make their own roads and fences. The huts are
made of bamboos, wattled with long grass, and
thatched with the same material, with boughs laid
over them to guard them against the wind. The
buildings are extremely rude, but still more artistic
than those of the Gonds; and every house has always
a separate thatched enclosure for sheltering cattle,
while the fields are surrounded with high fences of
boughs and bamboos, to keep out the deer and
antelopes from the corn. Having been thieves and
robbers for centuries, the men are still very careful
in protecting their villages, and the approach of a
stranger is always announced by a shrill scream,
which puts every one on his guard; and, unlike the
Gond fashion, their huts are always crowded close
together, as if for mutual protection. But they are
not inhospitable, and, merry of heart and unused to
the bonds of society, receive every wayfarer with a
gaiety peculiar to them, and are always assiduous in
making him comfortable. The chief defects still
observable in their character are that, though restless
and active, they are very impatient, and will stick to
no continuous work if they can do without it. They
are full of life and spirits, and will rove or hunt
through their forests all day, or commit the most
daring robberies in those parts of the country where
such things can yet be perpetrated with impunity;
but still they will rather live on half rations in

idleness than on a full diet with labour. They are also
excessively fond of liquor and tobacco, their favourite
beverage being a spirit distilled from the *mohwa*
flower, which is freely supplied to them by the enterprising Pársee, who has shops for vending it even in
the wilderness, and sells it for grain, grass, wood, or
anything that his customers will pay. The tobacco is
smoked rolled up in the form of a cigar inside the
leaf of the *áptá* tree, and the smoking is almost
continuous. They are, moreover, very filthy caters,
like the Gonds, and, though their staple food is maize
and rice, they reject nothing, devouring meat of all
kinds with eagerness, including that of foxes, jackals,
and snakes, and often when in a putrid state. Many
of them have become farmers, but are hardly even
now well reconciled to the change; some are hunters
by necessity; others live almost entirely on the
produce of their forests: what they are all equally apt
for yet is leading the same wild life that originally
belonged to them, notwithstanding the timidity
the plain Bheels seemingly evince. Much has been
already done to civilise them, and the amelioration
system is still being worked out; but it almost seems
that if they were left to themselves for a few years
it would not cost them much to relapse to their
old habits and ways. When trusted they are the
trustiest of men, and as a rule they are preferred
to other wild tribes generally for service in the
police and in gentlemen's houses; but the occasional

excesses they even now commit indicate clearly what they would be again if they could have their own way as before.

Among the redeeming features of the Bheel character are: great attachment for home and family, kindness towards women, respect for their elders, and an unsophisticated love for truth. A Bheel will never tell a lie; and he is generally so simple-hearted that, on being apprehended as an offender, he will not only confess all his transgressions, past and present, but will betray all his accomplices. As regards the position of the Bheel elders, the oldest man in each village is still always looked up to as its chief, and vested with a sort of patriarchal authority over the other villagers, which he exercises, however, by sufferance only, not by right; and, similarly, the domestic virtues are generally well cultivated, but without the ties being strongly and lawfully bound. The selection of a wife is always made by every Bheel himself, after which he enters into a formal engagement with the girl chosen at the foot of the *singd* tree, which is held to be particularly sacred; but there are no ceremonies of any kind to give validity to the engagement. When the marriage-day is fixed, the female relatives of the bridegroom force themselves into the house of the bride, and carry her off *vi et armis;* and, on her being brought to her lover, the marriage ceremony is com pleted, usually with a feast. But the parties thus united are not irrevocably bound. Generally they love each other, and the Bheel husband has always had the credit of allowing his wife to domineer over him. But they live in concert so long only as they choose, and separate at pleasure or convenience, the grown-up children being left with the father, while the younger ones are carried away by the mother. Polygamy is also practised, which necessarily qualifies the love of the husband for his wife; and, where there are several wives, the family house is seldom an abode of peace. As to religion, the ideas of the Bheels are based mainly on Hinduism, though not conforming to it very loyally. The chief deities recognised by the mountain tribes are named Sudál Deo, Kumbáh Deo, and Mámniá Dánip; the first of whom is worshipped in conjunction with the Sun and the Moon, and is supposed to have the elements under his control; the second, at the *Dewáli*, acting apparently as a substitute for the goddess Káli; while the third is the Ceres of the mountains—the dispenser of the bounties of the earth, at whose shrine the first fruits of the season are offered. We read, also, that the Ághori worship of Devi, in her most terrific forms, was at one time constantly celebrated by the mountaineers, and was always accompanied by human sacrifices, the *Vrihat Kathá* being full of stories on the subject, all the scenes describing which are laid in the Vindhyá range. Like the Gonds, however, the Bheels have no temples to worship their gods in, the usual place of worship being the foot of a large tree, where the objects of adoration are represented by big stones placed on a platform of mud. Adoration is also offered by them to their ancestors, the tiger, and the infernal spirits, the last of whom especially are very much feared; and sacrifices are likewise made to several of the minor Hindu deities to propitiate their favour. Witchcraft and omens, too, are believed in, as they are by almost all the wild tribes; and the *Holi* and the *Dasahára* are celebrated as affording opportunities for a debauch. There is usually a debauch also over the dead, of whom the males are burnt along with their arms and cooking utensils; while the females and children are buried, and a cairn of stones heaped over each grave.

THE KOLIS.

The Bheels extend westward to Guzerát, where they meet the Kolis, just as they extend eastward to Gondwáná, where they touch the Gonds. The especial seat of the Kolis is the country north of the river Máhee, the bulk of the population along the entire north-west frontier of Guzerát being also formed of them. They are a robust and bold-looking people, having the same physical peculiarities as the Bheels, and were long equally well known as enterprising thieves and plunderers, possessed of many hill-forts, which were all dismantled after the great Mahratta war. The Bheels regard them as being of

the same family with themselves; but the Kolis do
not acknowledge the relationship.   Living side by
side with each other, the character and habits of the
two races are naturally identical to a considerable
extent; but the Kolis, having become Hinduised to a
greater degree, consider themselves to be of higher
caste, and, though they do not object to marry Bheel
women, will not allow their own women to marry with
the Bheels.   There is otherwise so little difference
between them that Bishop Heber thought that the
Kolis were only civilised Bheels, who had laid
aside some of the wilder habits of their ancestors,
and sobered down to their present state.   But this
inference can hardly be justified, for the Kolis have
been generally recognised as the original inhabitants
of Guzerát, which the Bheels were not; and, as regards
wildness of character, the former have always shown
themselves to be a shade bloodier and more untame-
able even than the latter.   Of both races the wilder
tribes are still predatory where they can manage
to be so with impunity; and they are certainly
equally averse to honest labour and industry.   Though
claiming to be Hindus, the Kolis eat animals and
vermin of all kinds, like the Bheels, excepting the cow
and the village hog; nor object to do so when they
have died a natural death.   They are also inveterate
drunkards, and addicted to the use of opium and
bháng; and, in short, have all the habits which
distinguish the most degraded specimens of the

human race, despising every approach to civilisation
and decency as indicative of cowardice. When the
whole of Guzerát was occupied by them, it was
extremely difficult for merchants and pilgrims to
pass through their country; and their raids on
fairs and religious gatherings are said to have been
incessant. They were also largely employed by
the native chiefs in desolating each other's territories,
and had the reputation of being the most formidable
perpetrators of gang-robbery. The arms borne by
them were the knife, and the bow and arrows, to
which swords and matchlocks were added by those
who employed them. At present the chief theatre
of their activity is the sea-coast, as far down almost
as Goá, where, until lately, they were employed in
fishing and piracy; but elsewhere they are seen
living peaceably, as part of the general population
around them. The chief tribes living near the sea
are: the Ráj Kolis, who are cultivators and labourers;
the Solesy Kolis, who are also agriculturists; the
Towkry Kolis, who cut bamboos for sale, and derive
their name from their occupation; the Dhour Kolis,
who live principally as labourers, but are better known
for their degraded habits; the Doongury Kolis, who
are similarly employed and characterised; the Mullár
Kolis, who form the most respectable of all the septs,
and subsist chiefly by supplying villagers and wayfarers with water and other conveniences; the Áheer
Kolis, who are herdsmen, as the name implies; the

Murvee Kolis, who are very like the Murvee Bheels, and live mainly as palankeen bearers and porters ; and the Sone Kolis, who are fishermen and pirates. The chief tribes in Guzerát are called : the Tullubdáh, Pultunwárriá, Kákrez, Dháundhám, and Bábriáh Kolis, of whom the first are the most numerous, and superior to the others in rank. They are all agriculturists, and grow wheat, *dál*, maize, sugar-cane, and vegetables in large quantities, and rice also, of which the finer kinds are sold to the grain-merchants, while the coarser kinds are consumed by themselves. Their women work with them in the fields, and, though naturally well formed, are so hard worked as soon to lose all traces of their comeliness. The religion professed by them is Hinduism, all the gods of which are venerated and worshipped ; and the charms and amulets worn by the Hindus are also in common use among them.

THE GRÁSSIÁS

The Grássiás are another wild people belonging to Guzerát, and are also found in Málwá, in both of which places they were at one time noted for their robberies. They have no claim to the distinction of tribe or caste, being the refuse of all tribes, and derive their name from the free lands which were held by their ancestors. The Bheels and other jungle robbers having greatly disturbed the country by their

incursions, the Nawábs of Surát, in the reign of
Ferokesere, submitted to a compromise with them,
and ceded certain lands in each village which were
denominated *todd gyrdus*, or exempt from taxation.
The holders of these estates enlisted banditti of every
caste and country around them, and the descendants
of these robbers are the Grássiás. The main divisions
among them now are: the Rájpoot and Mahomedan
Grássiás respectively—the former sub-divided into
two tribes, named the Jhárejás and the Wagelás, and
the latter into ten or twelve tribes. The Rájpoot
tribes are, both of them, very ignorant and indolent,
and destitute alike of spirit and honour, and even of
jealousy for their feudal rights and privileges, their
whole time being taken up with sensual pleasures
and the most injurious abuse of intoxicating drugs
and liquors. Of the Mahomedan Grássiás there is
nothing particular to notice.

THE KÁTTIS.

A more prominent tribe in Western India are the
Káttis, who form the majority of the inhabitants of
Káttywár. Their name is derived from the word
kát, or wood, from which they affect to have been
produced. The story runs that a man sprang from
the rod of Karna—the half-brother and adversary of
the Pándavas—on its being split up, and that the
task of carrying off the cattle belonging to those

warriors from Berut, where they were living in privacy, was assigned to him. Kát was assured by Karna that the gods would never reckon robbery, and especially cattle-lifting, as a sin in him and his descendants, and the Káttis thus claim a divine ordinance and privilege to steal. Some writers affect that they are the same as the Cathaei who opposed the progress of Alexander in the Punjáb. They are certainly a large, well-formed race, athletic and bony, with expressive but harsh features, fair hair and complexion, and light-blue eyes, totally dissimilar in their appearance to the Kolis and the Bheels. Their women are proverbially beautiful, though almost masculine in size and make, while those of the Bheels, if not of the Kolis also, are ugly; and the legend is right in giving them a foreign descent from the earlier Scythians, which Karna and the Pándavas were. But they are outlaws all the same, and attach no disgrace or reproach to the mode of life they have always followed. Originally, they seem to have been of pastoral habits, and lived on the great wastes of Western India in hordes with their flocks; but even then their chief occupations were rapine and plunder. They had chiefs of their own to lead them, and gave asylum to outlaws of every description, whom they employed as mercenaries, not being a numerous tribe themselves. They paid these associates liberally, but never allowed them a share in the robbery, the profit and loss of every adventure being always their own; and they acquired large possessions in this way during the general anarchy produced by the decline of the Mahomedan power. It is scarcely three hundred years since they have settled in villages and betaken to fixed pursuits. As seen at present, almost every Kátti village has from two to four hundred goats, and sheep, cows, and buffaloes in proportion. The people were averse to cultivation before, but have betaken to that also gradually. But the occupation most pleasant to all of them is the breeding of horses—and they were at one time particularly formidable from the excellence of the horses they bred, when, well mounted and lance in hand, they collected black-mail alike from friend and foe. These horses were never shod, but yet travelled at great speed over the most stony countries without laming. No native robber, in fact, ever considers himself safe over a shod horse, for, if a shoe falls off, he is sure to be taken, since no horse accustomed to shoes can travel without them.

At this moment the Káttis are shepherds, cultivators, and thieves, by turns or together, as suits them best, and not less inclined to brigandage than before, if not strictly looked after; but they are more civilised than the Bheels and Kolis, large-hearted and hospitable, and keenly alive to their honour. Though treacherous to each other, they will never betray their guests. Their dress is decent, very much like that

of the Rájpoots, except that their turbans have peaks
or bills. Their arms are also the same with those in
general use in Rájpootáná, except that for a long
time they considered it disgraceful and a proof of
cowardice to carry firearms, and did not carry even
a shield with them. Though not numerous themselves, the tribal divisions among them are many, four
of whom only are important—namely, the Wálá, the
Khachur, and the Khoomán, who are termed "noble,"
and the Ehwarutiás, who are termed "ignoble," the
usages among whom are different in several respects.
The chief divinity recognised by all the tribes is the
Sun; but they have little sense of religion, and · no
prayers—their worship consisting simply of looking at
the luminary and invoking his favour. They have
priests, whose functions, however, are confined to the
ceremonies of marriage and *shrád.* Great reliance is
placed by them in omens, and much respect shown
to persons skilled in divination. Marriages are
celebrated by them in the same manner as by
the Hindus, with this difference, that, when the
bridegroom proceeds to the village of the bride to
marry her, his entrance is strongly opposed by her
friends, two courses only being left to him—namely,
either to force his way in, if he can, or to cry *peccavi,*
when he is admitted at once with a small following,
the rest of his friends being left in the cold, or taken in
after further palaver, after which the usual ceremonies
are proceeded with. In times past these fights for

a wife were often real trials of strength and courage not unattended with danger; but that character of them has long worn off. The re-marriage of widows is freely permitted and availed of by the Kattis, the widow of an elder brother always becoming the wife of a younger brother, though the widow of a younger brother can never be taken by an elder brother. As a rule, the men are much under the authority of their wives, being more henpecked than any other race in India. Like the other tribes near them, they are very fond of spirituous liquors and opium, and take both to excess; and on festive occasions there is no check to their intoxication, except what their wives may choose to exercise over them.

THE KATTOURIES.

We may also notice in this place the Kattouries, or Kattkuries, who occupy that part of the northern Konkan which lies along the base of the Sáhyádri range, and prepare catechu from the *khyre* tree. They profess to be descended from Rávana, King of *Lanká*, the counterfoil hero of the *Rámáyana*, and are said to have settled in their present quarters when the country was a wilderness. They are nomads in habit, and frequently change their place of residence—without, however, passing beyond the limits of the country they have hitherto possessed. The main tribal divisions among them are four—namely, Helum,

Jádoo, Powár, and Sindhi—the first being considered
the most important and respectable, and the last the
most degraded, while the third are probably identical
with the Powerá Bheels. All the septs are exceedingly
indolent and improvident, and, being more or less
filthy, live almost as outcasts in the places they
occupy, having their residences near, but never within,
the villages inhabited by other tribes. During the
hot weather and the rains they usually work as
labourers, grass-cutters, and firewood-sellers ; but at
all other times they repair to the jungles to
prepare catechu, taking up their residence frequently
in the sandy bed of a *nulláh*, where they sleep at
night. The catechu is prepared by bits of the *khyre*
tree being boiled with water, which is thickened
and on being cooled becomes firm. Large sums of
money are received by them for the preparation from
the merchants ; but these are even more easily
squandered than earned—after which the usual food
of the people consists again, as before, of the coarsest
roots and vegetables, and the flesh of such animals
and vermin as they can procure, including lizards,
rats, jackals, and serpents. They are also much
addicted to drink, and will frequently pawn their
rags for a dram, and then go naked from want. The
men have a squalid and half-starved appearance, and
the women are scarcely better looking, but are still
said to have great authority over their husbands.
Their temper, however, is untractable, which gives

rise to much disturbance in the family; and the
character of the tribe generally is very low, the
men being spoken of as thieves and robbers, and
tho women unchaste. The religion followed by them
is Hinduism, the deities particularly worshipped being
Bhairo, Bápdeo, Cheerobá, and Bhavání.

CHAPTER III.

TRIBES OF RÁJPOOTÁNÁ AND THE INDIAN DESERT.

THE MAIRS AND MEENÁS.

NORTH of the Bombay country, in the Arávulli mountains, live the Mairs and the Meenás, who are supposed to be of the same race, and had a history of their own in the past. The place is called *Mairwárá*, and stands as a rampart of hills, rising from 3000 to 4000 feet above the sea, and measuring a length of about 90 miles and a breadth of from 6 to 20 miles, from Guzerát on one side to near the Jumná on the other. The Mairs claim descent from Prithu Ráj of Delhi, and are therefore not a very old race, having branched out of the Meenás, the primeval denizens of Rájasthán. The story is that a son of Prithu took to himself a girl of the Meenás, and that the children born of the union became the fathers of the Mair tribe, the object aimed at being to establish a Rájpoot descent, even at the expense of legitimacy of birth. The original race was subdivided into five great tribes, that ruled

over the whole of Rájpootáná, from the Káli Koh
to the Jumná, in great strength and for a long
period, during the disturbances of the first Mahomedan dynasties of Delhi, to the mortification of
the Rájpoots. Eventually they were ousted from
their possessions and driven to the mountains, at
about the time when Báber invaded India; but the
constant internal dissensions that raged in Rájwárá
subsequently gave them incessant opportunities to
depredate on the States that surrounded them, and all
the efforts of the latter to subdue them were signally
unsuccessful. "Where hill joins hill," sung Chund,
the Hindu poet-laureate of Delhi, "the Mairs and the
Meenás are thronged to oppose the advance of the
Choháns;" and they maintained this attitude almost
throughout the whole of the Mahomedan era, alternately succumbing and depredating, and always
fighting with their Rájpoot suzerains. Their powers
of annoying with impunity were based on their habits
of life and the locality occupied by them; and the
state of the country was then much too troubled for
any effectual endeavour being made to reduce them.
The ostensible occupation followed by them was
that of goatherds; but the herds were usually left to
the charge of their boys and old men, while the
more able-bodied spent their time, mounted on their
diminutive and much-enduring ponies, in marauding,
plundering, and murdering. They had more than
fifty strongholds, or *kotes*, to operate from; and the

haughty Rájpoots were obliged to pay black-mail to them to purchase their forbearance. The detriment to trade became so great at last that the Rájpoot States were forced to combine together to beat up their hills and jungles; but they were not finally reduced till 1820, when their country was occupied by the British army then operating in Rájasthán. Mair-wárá had been ceded to the British Government previously by Dowlut Ráo Scindiáh, in 1818; but, the States of Oodypore and Jodhpore having claimed rights over some portions of it at this time, nothing was done in it till the later date mentioned, when its entire management was transferred into British hands. Of the steps then taken to reduce the Mairs into obedience and order the most important was, as in Bheelwárá, the formation of a local corps, which converted the freebooters into soldiers, by whom the rest of the people were forcibly reclaimed. The condition of the country has since been comparatively prosperous, cultivation in it having in particular most enormously increased.

The unmixed or Meená race is now exceedingly rare; but the mixed Mair race is found spread over all the hilly parts of Rájwárá as plentifully as before. Previous to the establishment of the British power among them they used to live generally in conceal-ment among their rugged hills, hardly wearing any clothing, and practising no useful occupation besides herding. Their habits have so far changed that they all put on a loin-cloth and a *chádur* now, after the same fashion as the Bhcels; and, the plan of living by plundering. only having become obsolete, they have been obliged to become cultivators to a great extent, while some have taken service as soldiers under the paramount power. In their native fast-nesses there are, of course, some Mairs yet almost as wild and ferocious as they ever were, who continue to hold the Rájpoots of the plains in utter contempt, and are known all over Upper India principally as dacoits; but even these are coming round gradually, and, having commenced to intermarry with the Ráj-poots, are shaping their manners and customs after them. They all profess to be Hindus, with the exception of those who have become Mahomedans, and their marriage and other ceremonies are con-ducted in Rájpoot fashion; but they are not over scrupulous in the observance of the tenets they profess, and, in the matter of food especially, are not very particular. They eat the flesh of sheep, cows, and buffaloes without hesitation, and even when the animals have died of disease, but refrain from the flesh of hogs and fowls. Strong drinks are also indulged in by them, but very seldom to excess. Two revolting customs had existed long among them—namely, infanticide and the sale of women—which are believed to have since died out. Widow-marriage is very common with them, and also divorce, even more than among the Bheels. If tempers do not agree, or other causes prompt them to part, the husband tears a shred from his turban and gives it to his wife, and, with this deed of separation in her hand, and placing two jars of water on her head, she takes whatever path she pleases, and the first man who chooses to ease her of the jars becomes a new husband unto her. Another peculiarity of the tribe is that they do not tolerate the residence of aliens amongst them, and are necessarily obliged to subdivide themselves into the classes of cultivators, artificers, and servants, having thus their own smiths, carpenters, potters, barbers, *chámárs*, and minstrels. The arms used by the Mairs are the sword, shield, ahd spear or javelin. Their old rules prohibited them from robbing a Bráhman, a woman, and a *fakir*, and it is said that these are yet rigidly adhered to.

THE DESERT TRIBES.

In the Indian desert lying between Rájwárá and the Indus the principal wild tribes, after the Bheels, Kolis, and Mairs, are the Sodás, Kaorwás, Dháttis, Lohannás, Rebárris, and Sehráes, who may be very shortly described in this place.

THE SODÁS.

The Sodás profess to be of Rájpoot descent, and at one time their power all over the desert border was very great. But they have long lost their original name for courage, and are now chiefly known as dexterous thieves only. Their arms are the sword, the shield, and a long knife worn in the girdle. The primitive sling is also used by them, and with great expertness. Their general condition is very barbarous; but they are rich in herds of camels, oxen, and goats, the milk of which affords them a plentiful and nutritious fare, varied with the flesh of their goats on particular occasions. The jungles of the desert, moreover, yield them wild vegetables of various kinds, and with these comforts they are generally contented and happy.

THE KAORWÁS.

The Kaorwás are nomadic, and have no fixed place to live in. They are constantly moving about with their flocks, and encamp wherever they can find a spring and pasture for them, where they improvise temporary huts for their own accommodation, under some wide-spreading tree, in such skilful manner that the existence of any habitation there cannot easily be detected. Their habits are peaceful, and they are more frequently the victims of outlaws than outlaws themselves. They rear camels, cows, buffaloes, and goats, and sell them to merchants and others; and this is the only occupation they live by.

THE DHÁTTIS.

The Dháttis are very like the Kaorwás—that is, also of pastoral and peaceful habits. They cultivate to a small extent, but so rudely as virtually to leave

it to nature to raise the crops. Their supply of food-
grains is more certainly acquired by bartering the
ghee derived from their flocks, which helps them to
secure many other necessaries of life also. Their
chief fare consists of porridge and buttermilk, and,
the cows of the desert being much larger than those
of the plains, the produce of three or four cows is
sufficient to supply all the requirements of a large
family by the sale of *ghee*.

THE LOHANNÁS.

The Lohannás form a numerous tribe, and are
principally of commercial habits. They are said to
be of Afghán descent, but wear the Bráhmanical
string, or *junoee*, and are perhaps the only race
of Mahomedans who affect to be Hindus. They
conduct the main portion of the traffic between India
and the countries beyond the Indus. Their habits
are necessarily migratory; but they are otherwise not
very wild at present, being apt scribes and shop-
keepers. In the matter of food only they are as
omnivorous and undiscriminating as any of the other
tribes named, not stopping at anything except their
cats, dogs, and cows; and they drink spirituous
liquors also to an immoderate extent.

THE REBÁRRIS.

The Rebárris are shepherds, goatherds, and camel-
breeders, and have a name for stealing camels, in

which they are said to be very dexterous. When any of them comes upon a herd of camels grazing, he strikes his lance at the first animal he reaches, and, dipping a cloth with its blood, thrusts it close to the nose of the next animal, and wheeling about sets off at speed, upon which he is pursued by the whole herd, the leader of which is lured by the scent of the blood, and is followed by the rest. The life of the race is almost purely rural, and in general habits they resemble the Sodás more than any other tribe. They have usually many wives; and their women are not ill-looking.

THE SEHRÁES.

The Sehráes are a large race, and have sub-divisions named the Kossál, Chándiá, and Sudáni. They form altogether the principal robber tribe of the desert; and their bands are mostly mounted on horses or camels, and are armed with lances of bamboo and iron, and swords and shields. Of late years they have reduced their modes of rapine to a system, and are content to levy black-mail—paid either in money or grain—for every plough working within their reach; and it is exceedingly difficult to elude them.

THE THORI.

There are many other tribes in the desert, most of whom are of Beloochee descent. One of these, the Thori, have the distinctive epithet of *Bhoot*, or devil, applied to them, and are also called "the sons of the devil." They are so reckless and so entirely destitute of moral sense that they will not hesitate even to bring a man's head to his enemy for the most trifling remuneration; and this is the general character of the rest.

CHAPTER IV.

THE KOLARIAN AND OTHER RACES IN BENGAL.

THE country called Chotá Nágpore terminates the plateau of Central India on the east, and is connected, by a continuous chain of hills, on one side, with the Vindhyá and Kymore ranges, and, on another, with the highlands of Amarkantak. The average elevation of the tract is about 2,000 feet above the sea, and here the Kolarian races, fleeing before their conquerors, seem to have taken their final stand. Of the separate names by which those races were distinguished, the best known now are the Koles and the Sonthals; but they all formed a kindred people at one time, by whom the Bráhman onset Bengalwards seems to have been most vigorously opposed. They were finally defeated, broken up, and scattered; upon which they settled in different parts of the Chotá Nágpore Division, and in the Tributary Estates of Chotá Nágpore and Cuttack. Alongside of them, but as a distinct race, are found the Oráons, another aboriginal race, who, though not of the Kolarian

type, appear to have shared with the Koles the glory
of having best resisted the Bráhmans. The story of
the Oráons is that they came to Chotá Nágpore after
the Koles, agreeing to occupy the place jointly with
them without fighting, under the condition of mutual
help against a common enemy ; and they both differ
almost equally in all respects from the people of the
plains, at the same time that they are distinguished
from one another by features peculiar to each. Their
country was a jungle when they came to it ; they
have converted it into a garden ; and the praise is
due in the same degree to both.

THE KOLES.

The Koles are a numerous people, divided into
several tribes, among whom are the Moondás, the
Larkás, the Hos, the Chooárs, and the Bhoomij.
They occupy all the country from the jungles of
Rámgurh, near Házáreebágh, to the south and
southward, down to the confines of Gángpore and
Sirgoojá; but those dwelling in Singbhoom, a portion
of which is called the *Kolehán*, are the best known.
The original inhabitants of the Kolehán were the
Bhooyáns, an extremely simple and inoffensive
people, who were excellent cultivators and rich in
cattle, and by whom the Koles, when they came
in, were invited to settle at their side. The two
races went on very peacefully together in this state
of pristine love till some Márwáree adventurers,

journeying through their country, incited the Koles
to get up a quarrel with the Bhooyáns, upon which
the latter removed themselves to Porahát, Bondi,
and other places lying on the way from Orissá to
Behár, where they have become almost completely
Hinduised, though still leading the same simple,
harmless, and unsophisticated life as before. Where
the Koles came from cannot now be very easily
explained, for the race is a widely diffused one, of
which branches are met with almost in every direction.
If they be identical with the Kolis of Western India,
or of common descent with them, there is, as was first
pointed out by Sir George Campbell, in his *Ethnology
of India*, a hiatus of four or five degrees of longitude
now between the two septs, caused probably by the
Gonds having forcibly intervened between them.
Tribes having similar names are also to be found
in other places, though the characteristics by which
they are severally distinguished are not identical.
After their settlement in the Kolchán, the Rájpoots
for a long series of years claimed a sort of authority
over the Koles, which, however, was never acknowledged by them, and the Rájáh of Chotá Nágpore
attempting to enforce it gave rise to the insurrection
of 1819-20 in Palámow. There was a second insurrection in 1831, which, originating in Chotá Nágpore,
spread rapidly all over the districts of Singbhoom,
Rámgurh, Toree, and Palámow; and this also was a
rising more against the zemindárs than against the

Government. One general cause of it was the
cruelty of the zemindárs, who extorted *ábwábs*
(presents) at will, which the Koles were unable to pay
easily, severely punishing those who resisted; and
another, the transfer of lands from the possession
of men descended from the original settlers of the
soil to alien proprietors, under a farming lease. A
specific case of oppression especially resented was
this, that a particular zemindár had given farms
of some villages to certain Sikh and Mahomedan
adventurers over the heads of the Kole chiefs or
Mánkis, and that, the latter having been dispossessed,
their women were abused and ill-treated. Generally
an inoffensive people, the Koles became wild with
excitement over this question, and rose in a body to
resist. They would not forego their rights, and did
not understand the legal quibbles by which those
rights were said to have been forfeited. The ill-treat-
ment of their women was naturally another sore
point with them, and they assembled together and
planned a general revolt. "We have been cheated
and dishonoured," said the different tribes to each
other; "we are brethren, and must fight together
for revenge." Arrows were circulated like the fiery
cross among their people in all places, and they rose
everywhere to plunder, burn, and kill. A discreet
magistrate might have settled matters even at this
stage without difficulty; but there was no such officer
on the spot. The Koles were opposed as rebels, and,

as they showed themselves to be not unworthy of their descent from the hardy *Dasyas* who had resisted the Bráhmans, their whole country had to be swept from one extremity of it to the other before the insurrection could be extinguished. This done, the grievances they complained of were attended to and redressed, by the revenue administration being reorganised so as to restore the Mánkis to authority and deprive the zemindárs of the power to oust them; and since then, by a re-settlement in 1867, the management of the Kolchán has been directly assumed by the officers of the Government.

The Koles are a fine people—much finer than the other cognate tribes around them. They are of a black colour, like the rest, and their countenances are not well-favoured; but they are hardy and athletic, have an erect and easy carriage and long free strides, and their hands and feet are both large and well-formed. The hair is worn long, and combed and oiled, alike by the males and the females; but the former shave the forehead, which contributes greatly to their ugliness. Clothing is regarded as a superfluity by them, and even the rich have only a narrow *dhoti* and a *dopuṭṭá*, which is gladly thrown by except on state occasions. Of the lower orders the women prefer to go naked, or simply pass the *kopni* between their legs and fasten it before and behind to a string wound round the waist; but those of the higher orders have already taken to tasteful *sárees*, and look

handsome in them. In all places the want of clothing
hitherto arose mainly from the art of weaving being
unknown to them; but this difficulty is being removed
by the introduction of foreign weavers into their
country. The ornaments worn by the women are
ear-rings and immense bunches of bead necklaces, of
which they are very fond. The men also wear
ear-rings, and necklaces of small beads with charms
against snakes, tigers, and diseases depending from
them. Their arms are the bow and arrows, and the
battle-axe called *tángi;* and in times past they led
bloody forays, in which a large amount of violence was
committed. At present all their vigour is expended
on field-sports, of which they are passionately
fond; and among some tribes, such as the Moondás
and the Hos, even young boys are trained up as
shikáries, and are to be seen stalking about birds'
nests with bows and arrows. The implements which
are now most generally in use, however, among all the
tribes are those used in agriculture—namely, the
plough, the harrow, the sickle, and the *koddli* or big
hoe; and they plough with cows as well as with
bullocks, which is natural to a people making no
use of milk. The whole of the Kolehán is extremely
fertile and well watered, and three crops of rice are
raised in it annually, besides which they cultivate
maize, millet, wheat, pulses, mustard, tobacco, and
cotton. They take great interest also in farming;
and a vast number of sheep, goats, and cattle are

bred, and the milk and *ghee* of the cattle are sold in great quantities for the most trifling prices. Ducks, geese, and poultry are also reared, and animal food of all kinds is eaten, beef and hog's flesh included; but, unlike other tribes in their neighbourhood, they do not eat bears, monkeys, field-mice, and snakes. They have no caste prejudices, and eat rice by whomsoever it may be cooked; but they have their own peculiar superstitions, and will leave off eating if a man's shadow passes across the dish, and never drink water from an earthen vessel touched by any other tribe. They are passionately fond of dancing, and have a great variety of dances, which they perform with precision; and little children hardly on their legs begin to learn the dancing-steps. This exhibits them as a light-hearted and good-natured race; but there is another side of the picture which is not equally flattering. They are exceedingly indolent, so much so that their women have to perform all the hardest duties of the field; immoderately dirty, and, except in the hot season, will seldom touch water; and inordinately fond of drink, which accounts for the *soondis* being seen in shoals throughout their country, it being a common saying among themselves that on marriage and other festive occasions they get so drunk that servants forget their duty to their masters, children their reverence for their parents, men their respect for women, and women their respect for decency. They are also extremely

F

sensitive, which makes cases of suicide very common among them. But they are, on the other hand, very manly and honest; and, even when they were living by plunder and violence, lying, deceit, and pilfering were never laid to their charge. The truth of the men and the modesty of their women have, in fact, been always proverbial; and it frequently happens that when a man has committed a crime, far from attempting to conceal it, he comes forward unasked and surrenders himself red-handed for punishment.

The villages of the Koles are of small size and irregular shape, but generally situated prettily on the hills, so as to overlook their flat-terraced rice-fields and undulating uplands. The irregularity in form arises from the houses being distinct from each other, and hedged in by their own little plots of cultivation respectively; and the size is not extensive because of the dislike of the people to congregate from fear of fires and contagious diseases. The consequence is that almost every crest of ground in the country has been converted into a village, but each consisting of a few scattered huts only. None of the villages are ever built by river sides, and the women have necessarily to draw water from great distances. The houses of the nomad Koles are, for the most part, small and miserable, being temporary, as they are always looking out for fresh clearings in the forests; but those of the stationary tribes, and especially of their chiefs, are always substantial, roomy, and well made, and usually built so as to enclose a square, often having also a verandá to boast of. The compartments are ordinarily three in number—namely, for sleeping, eating, and keeping stores in respectively; and opposite to each house, at a distance of about thirty paces, there is always another for accommodating servants, wayfarers, and guests, the flanks of the two being joined by cow-houses, granaries, and pig-styes. Among the Larkás, the most powerful tribe of all, the unmarried young men are not allowed to sleep in the family-house at night; but this custom is not observed by the Moondás, Hos, and other tribes, among whom all the members of a family live together at all hours. Over love-making and free intercourse there are no restrictions at all. The girls have their prices fixed on them, which their lovers must pay before the consent of their parents to their marriage can be obtained; but no other impediment intervenes, and, if matters go too far between any particular couple, the case is usually settled by the lover being made to pay the girl's price and to marry her. The selection in every case is made by the parties concerned, but has to be finally ratified by their parents as a matter of form. The marriage ceremony is very simple. After everything has been settled, the bride is led to the bridegroom's house and seated on a *mord* of *dhán*, when oil is poured on her head, and boiled rice and meat are offered to her, by partaking of which she becomes

of her husband's caste. There is next a dance in the
nearest grove, in which the cortége on both sides take
part; a cup of beer is then given to each of the
lovers, and the liquor of the two cups being mixed is
drunk up by both, which completes the rite. After
remaining three days with her husband, the most
modest course for the wife to follow is to run away
from his house and tell her friends that she cannot
love him; and the husband must show great anxiety
for her, find her out, and carry her back by force,
when she becomes settled with him for good. Wives
are very well treated by the Koles, and necessarily so,
because they work very hard' for their husbands. A
Kole wife is invariably her husband's companion, and
is consulted by him in all his difficulties; and this is
especially so among the Hos. She is not subjected
to any restraint whatever, and infidelity on her part
is very rare. Where it does occur the unfaithful wife
is discarded, and her seducer has to refund to her
husband the price he paid for her. Polygamy is
permitted, but is seldom availed of. The religion
of the Koles is based on the belief of a Supreme
Being named Sing Bongá, who is represented by the
Sun. The Moon is believed to be his wife, and the
Stars his daughters. Besides these there are a herd
of local and sylvan gods; but of none are images made,
nor is any sort of worship known beyond sacrifices.
Every village has a grove attached to it where the
sacrifices are performed; but the minor gods are

propitiated only as intercessors with Sing Bongá.
The appeals to them are constant in cases of sickness
and for good crops, and the sacrifices are always
accompanied by bacchanalian debaucheries. The
belief in omens and charms is also great, especially
among the tribes on the Sumbulpore frontier, who
have mixed much with the Gonds. All the Koles
burn their dead on the pyre, with their ornaments,
arms, and raiment on. The half-consumed bones are
then taken out of the ashes and put into an earthen
vessel, which is buried along with rice, clothes, and
money, and a stone is placed over the spot; and
close to Chyebássá, on the road to Keonjhur, a group
of cenotaphs is seen, some of them built with very
big stones.

THE SONTHÁLS.

The Sonthális are a nomad race, believed, like
the Koles, to have emigrated from the northern
parts of India. They occupy all the western jungles
of Bengal, particularly those of Rewáh, Palámow,
Házáreebágh, Chotá Nágpore, Mánbhoom, and Cuttack; and yet more especially those at the foot of
the Rájmahal hills, where the tract inhabited by them
is called *Sonthálid*, or the Sonthál Pergunnáhs. The
district lies between Behár and Bengal, and has the
shape of an angle doubled by the Ganges as it passes
down from the first province into the second. It
forms at the present day the most important of all

the Sonthál settlements, though it was apparently
not one of their original seats, the traditions of the
race speaking of it as one of the last places they
inhabited in their wanderings. It is subdivided into two
distinct parts—namely, an inner territory about 1,400
square miles in extent, which is called the Dámun-i-
koh, and a second territory about 4,200 square miles
in extent, which surrounds the first, and seems to
have been later settled upon. Unlike the Koles,
the Sontháls care little to stick permanently at any
particular spot; and, as the Páháriáhs, who inhabit the
upper hills of the Dámun, were at all times content
with their summits, and repudiated the valleys and
the level lands lying beyond them, the Sontháls came
gradually to occupy them, from their fondness for
virgin ground. In course of time they increased in
numbers on the spot, both by birth and immigration;
and, when the clearances effected by them became
extensive, the Government was glad to settle the
lands with them. The Páháriáhs looked on these
advances with distrust, and at one time gave much
trouble to their neighbours in consequence; but they
have got cured of their predatory habits long since,
and the Sontháls have had no reason to complain of
them for many years past. Their later annoyances
came rather from the zemindárs and the *mahájuns*,
who managed between them to drive the Sontháls into
rebellion in 1854-55. The zemindárs, besides levying
their legitimate dues, exacted as much more as they

thought their ryots could be made to pay; and, what with *gumdstás, suburáKárs*, peons, and agents, false measures at *háts* and markets, and the wilful trespass of the rich on growing crops by letting in cattle on them, the system was felt as very oppressive by a simple-hearted people. To meet these extortions, the Sonthál was obliged to have recourse to the *mahájun*, who was ever ready to advance whatever sums were asked for. But the debts thus contracted could never be repaid. Paid ten times over, they still remained unliquidated; and the Sonthál's accounts of knots on a string invariably went to the wall against the account-books produced by the *mahájun* in court in support of his claim. "Do the *Sáhebs*, then, join with the *mahájuns* in cheating and oppressing us?" asked each Sonthál of his neighbour, in alarm. "What alternative is there, then, for us but to rebel?" And they rose in revolt, to resist both the *mahájuns* and the *Sáhebs*. The story of Sidhoo and Kánoo is well known. They proclaimed themselves to be messengers from heaven especially deputed to redress the wrongs of their race; and the Sontháls gathered around them in large numbers in arms. A police-dárogá, endeavouring to suppress the rising forcibly, was killed by Sidhoo, and, blood having been shed, the rebellion extended rapidly, with frightful atrocity. Troops poured in now into Sonthália from all sides; and, as the Sontháls would not yield, they had to be shot down in numbers, after which the country was

pacified. As in the Kolehán, a more genial administration was now given to it than it had possessed
before, whereby the systems of oppression it had
suffered from were swept away. From the direct
hearing of cases, speedy orders, expeditious appeals,
absence of interference on the part of the *āmlāh*, etc.,
the Sonthāls felt that their position was now very
much bettered, and quietly resumed the peaceful life
they had momentarily abandoned. A second rising
was threatened in the outer tract on a later day, on
account of the rack-renting practised there by the
zemindárs and ghátwáls; but this was averted by
the jungles of the tract being resumed by the
Government, and the entire area of the Sonthál
Pergunnáhs resettled on the ryotwary system—that
is, with the Sontháls.

The Sonthál is absolutely the best specimen of the
wild tribes in India. He is a short, well-made, and
active man, having a round face, and the thick lips,
high cheek-bones, and spread nose of the Gond,
Bheel, and Kole. He is beardless—or nearly so—
while the hair of his head is straight, coarse, and
black. In his dealings with other men he is shy, if
not cowardly; but he is very brave when confronted
with wild animals. He is a good hunter, a good
herdsman, and a good agriculturist; self-dependent in
everything and never idle, and necessarily almost
never in distress. His skill, patience, and diligence
are exemplary; and he has implements of his own

making and a peculiar system of cultivation which
enable him to cultivate very successfully, after his own
manner. He always reclaims the jungles he comes to
inhabit, and carefully collects all their products, which
he either sells or barters for other articles from his
neighbours; but he will do all this for himself and his
family only, and will never take service with any one.
If any attempt be made to coerce him he never thinks
of offering resistance, but decamps into the innermost
jungles, where it is impossible to follow him, and
where he commences new clearances on his own
account. Like the Kole, he is not a weaver himself,
but he has had weavers about him from a longer date,
and usually dresses better than the Kole, though his
working dress is often none other than the *kopni*,
or cloth passed between the legs and fastened to a
string worn round the loins. His wife makes a more
decent appearance at all times. She is short like her
husband, and plump, but has usually a pleasing
expression in her countenance; and her dress for
many years past has been the Bengali *sáree*, which
she wears in the same fashion as the Bengalis, except
that no part of it is used as a veil. The chief
ornaments in use among both sexes are flowers and
feathers, and also cowtail-hair necklaces, which are
very neatly manufactured. The women also wear on
their arms, ankles, and throats ornaments made of
brass and bell-metal, which are excessively heavy;
and the love of the husband is in this sense a sore

burden to the wife. The food of the Sonthál consists
principally of *janerd* and maize, accompanied with
eggs, poultry, and the flesh of goats, kids, or swine;
but he will eat anything besides that he can obtain,
and is not particular as to the hands they come
from, with one singular exception only. His antipathy
against the Hindu is so great that he will never eat
cooked food coming even from the hands of a
Bráhman, though there is no tradition to account
for the feeling, which has come down to him from
generation to generation, testifying to the existence
of some bitter feud between the races in the past.
The chief drink of the Sonthóls is the *pachwái*, or
fermented grain; but they do not drink so much as
the Koles, and their debauch is necessarily less to
that extent.

Though he is but a nomad in habits, the hut of the
Sonthál is well made, and well raised. Its walls are
made of matting, or hurdle, or thin sticks smeared
over with mud; and, owing to his love of colours, a
gay appearance is often given to them by their being
painted with different shades of red, white, and black,
according to the owner's fancy. The roof is of thatch,
and every hut is always roomy within, the Sonthál
having usually a large family to accommodate. Each
couple has an average of eight or nine children, and
the house is necessarily always full; but it is also
always clean, and has a tidiness in almost everything
about it. The arrangement of houses is such as to

form a long street through every village, one house
deep on each side; and each house has attached to
it a pig-sty and a dove-cot, besides which there are
buffalo-sheds scattered here and there, varying in
size according to the wealth of the inhabitants. The
villages are buried in thick jungle, but are not difficult
to find, being easily traceable by the small cleared
patches of ground to be found near them, which are
always pleasant to look at, and yet more by the music
proceeding from them at all times. The Sonthál is
an admirer of nature, and never fells down any useful
or ornamental tree, which gives his clearings a park-
like and unmistakable appearance; and he is Arcadian
in practice, and enjoys life better than other people of
the same grade, from being immensely fond of music
and dancing. His flute is a simple instrument made
of the bamboo, but gives out deep, rich tones; and
every village has a dancing-ground where the youths
and maidens meet in the evening to dance and sing.
This is the national custom, and no harm is thought
of it; and the maidens, decked with flowers and
feathers, pair off with the young men, all blithely
going round in a circle, with their feet falling in
cadence, and singing responsive to musicians placed
in their centre. That such freedom of intercourse
may not be abused, there is a *jóg-mánjee*, or censor,
in every village, to look after the morals of the
young, while another officer superintends all family
arrangements generally, and, with the aid of the

village priest, keeps matters straight. There is a
covered platform besides in each village, where the
head men meet to talk over and regulate village
affairs, and to award punishments where they may
have been deserved. All marriages in the Sonthál
country are said to be love-matches, though it is
considered respectable for the parents to mature the
necessary arrangements, as if without the knowledge
of the lovers. The selection is said to be preceded
by a beastly festival, named *Bandana*, which is held
in the month of January, and lasts for six days,
when all candidates for matrimony, male and female,
are assembled together and permitted to have
promiscuous intercourse with each other, each lover
selecting his future wife after the termination of this
general carnival. Polygamy is permitted, but is
seldom had recourse to; and the wife is always
treated with kindness. Divorces are also permitted
when man and wife find out that they are not suited
to each other, the order of separation being invariably
given by a *punchάyet*.

The tribal divisions of the Sontháls are: the Saran,
Murmu, Márli, Kisku, Besárá, Hánsdá, Tudí, Báski,
Hemroo, and Choráí; but they do not materially
differ from each other in any respect. The chief
god of all the tribes is Sing Bongá, the same as of
the Koles; and he is worshipped after the same
fashion also, namely, as the Sun God. Besides him
there are several minor gods and *bhoots* who have

to be propitiated ; and the spirit of Borá Mánjee, a deceased and canonised chief, is also venerated, and often invited by the initiated, by fasting and sacrifices, to answer references made to it in respect to village affairs. The Bágh-Bhoot, or tiger spirit, is another object of reverence ; and several tribes worship the living tiger as well as the *bhoot*. The women pay great respect likewise to the elephant, and touch the earth with their foreheads before him, praying him to bless their children, who are seated in perfect confidence at his feet. Of set celebrations one of the greatest is the hunting festival organised annually, which every adult has to join fully armed and accoutred. The arms of the Sonthals are the same as of the Gonds, Bheels, and Koles—namely, the battle-axe, and the bow and arrows ; and with these they go out to hunt in a body, pursuing wild animals of all kinds, except tigers and bears, which are never wantonly molested, though, if their path be crossed by either, they are not afraid to encounter them. The expedition lasts for four or five days, after which the game secured enables the party to celebrate a great feast, which the women are invited to join. Feasts on smaller scales are also celebrated on occasions of marriages and deaths. The dead among the Sonthals are burnt, as among the Koles ; but the ashes and bones, instead of being buried, are consigned to the currents of rivers held sacred after the Hindus.

THE ORÁONS.

The Oráons, better known as the Dhángurs, or hill-men, inhabit the north and west parts of the Chotá Nágpore district, and are also scattered over the other districts of the division, and over Sumbulpore. They have a tradition among them that they came originally from Konkan, and settled first at Rhotás, whence one party diverged to their present quarters, while another party, the Paháriáhs, occupied the Rájmahal hills. When they came to Chotá Nágpore the Koles of the Moondá tribe were already settled in it; but, being of a peaceful disposition, these offered no opposition to them, and the two races lived side by side in harmony together. As the Hindus spread and prevailed the Oráons were obliged to fly before them, and came thus to be diffused over all the country now occupied by them. The plateau of Chotá Nágpore which they inhabit is a magnificent place; but their life and appearance are not in keeping with the scenery. They are small-sized and ill-favoured ; and, though their young men give themselves a jaunty air and are very careful in decorating their persons, that does not exhibit them to greater advantage. They are of dark complexion, and have projecting jaws and thick lips, while their forehead is low and narrow, and their eyes are meaningless and vacant. The hair is worn long, and gathered into a knot behind,

which supports a red or white turban on gala days ;
but ordinarily there is a mirror and a comb stuck
into it, with bright buttons and chains having spiky
pendants dangling therefrom. Here the decorations
of the Oráons end, and even these are discarded after
marriage, which makes their subsequent appearance
unprepossessing and negligent. The only cloth worn
by them is a narrow strip wound round the loins,
and in the wilder parts of the country even this is
wanting, the *kopni*, or cloth passed between the legs,
being substituted for it. The men are, however,
always very good-humoured, and the women modest
in demeanour, though their dress, too, is scanty. In
some places the women have the usual *sáree* with red
border, which serves as a petticoat, and even a *chádur*
to put over the body; but in others the bandage
round the loins is their only clothing—worn longer,
however, than by the men. The ornaments of the
women consist of a large quantity of red beads and
heavy brass necklaces hung round the throat, and
rings of copper on the fingers and in the ears, besides
which they are tattooed all over the body—on the
forehead, arms, and back—even young men bearing
the marks on their forearms. One sign of civilisation
is certainly shown by the women : they wear false
hair to make up with their natural hair a chignon
of size, over which heron plumes are displayed on
festive occasions. Another test of civilisation (native)
is that the *soi-pátána* of Bengali women is understood

by them, and is named *gui*. When two girls feel a particular penchant for each other they swear eternal friendship and exchange necklaces, and the compact is witnessed by common friends. They do not name each other after this ratification of goodwill, but are " my flower," or " my *gui*," or " my meet-to-smile," to each other to the end of their lives.

The huts of the Oráons are badly built and huddled up, and are quite incapable of affording decent accommodation ; and the consequence is that the men and their cattle live, not only within the same compound, but often in the same apartment. The walls of the huts are of mud, and where constructed of red laterite earth are as durable as if built of brick and mortar. The accommodation being scanty, the young members of a family do not live with their parents, the bachelors of the village having a hall common to themselves, while the maidens are billeted with the widows, who, if not discreet, often allow them to mix freely with their lovers. The bachelors' hall has a dancing arena before it, where young men and girls meet frequently to amuse themselves; and, during the festive seasons, they often dance throughout the night, provided the supply of beer is sufficient to keep up the enjoyment so long. As a rule, however, boys and girls of the same village do not intermarry, it being considered more respectable to bring home a bride from a distance. The marriage of children is unknown ;

and, as among the Sonthâls, most of the marriages
are said to be love matches purely. The selection
of his wife is always made by the would-be husband
himself, after which his parents go through a form of
selection for him. When the time for the marriage
is settled, the bridegroom, with a party, proceeds to
the bride's village to bring her over; but she is not
surrendered before a mock fight with her friends,
who refuse to part with her. The fight eventually
ends in a dance, in which the bride and bridegroom
join. The marriage ceremony is called *sindoorddu*,
and is performed under a screen. The bride and
bridegroom are made to stand over a curry-stone,
the former being posted before the latter, and both
surrounded by their friends, while all intruders are
turned out. A cloth is then thrown over them, and
the man daubs the girl's head with *sindoor*, or
vermilion, while the girl returns the compliment by
just touching his brow without turning her head.
They are then bathed, and retire to a private apartment to change their clothes, from which they come
out sometime after, and are saluted man and wife.
Both man and wife live as labourers, and the race
is widely known as the chief labouring class of
Bengal. Many of them go out as emigrant coolies
to various parts of the world, and return with money
enough to maintain them in independence if they
could only husband their savings properly. But this
they never can; they spend in a month what would

G

make them comfortable for life, and then cheerfully return to work and privations. They believe that they were created for labour, and have a natural relish for it. Their work is enlivened with sports, and the men are quite as fond of field sports as the Moondás and the Hos, and are very successful hunters. Whatever they hunt they eat; but their chief food is rice and *dál*. They seldom use vegetables, and their cooking is so wretched that they could not possibly have made anything eatable out of them. Their religion, like that of the Koles and the Sonthals, recognises a Supreme God who is made manifest in the Sun; but they think it useless trouble to pray to him, as he does not send evil. There are malignant spirits who afflict mankind, and these have to be propitiated, since even the Sun-God cannot control them, or protect any one from their persecutions. The belief in ghosts, sorceries, and witchcrafts is also widely diffused; and there are two important functionaries in each village—the Maháto and the Páhn, or the secular administrator and the priest—whose chief duty is to look after and regulate the precautionary measures to be taken. They have no idea of futurity. Men killed by tigers become tigers, but for all others death is annihilation, excepting those who, dying under peculiar circumstances, become ghosts. The dead are burned, and the ashes and charred bones being collected are placed in an earthen vessel, which is kept suspended near the house of the deceased till the cold weather, when its contents are allowed to mix with the bones and ashes of his ancestors. The chief festivals of the Oráons are two, and both of them are agricultural—namely, the *Sarhul* festival, which solemnises the marriage of the earth, and the *Karma* festival, which celebrates a plentiful harvest.

THE PÁHÁRIÁHS.

The Rájmahál hills, we have said, are occupied by two distinct races—namely, the Páháriáhs, who inhabit the summit of the hills, and the Sonthals, who live at their foot and in the valleys. The hillmen are the original inhabitants, the Sonthals the interlopers; and the latter were frequently depredated upon by the former in times gone by. The character of the hillmen was utterly savage and cruel, and throughout the Mahomedan period they were the scourge and terror alike of the Sonthals and the surrounding country, while the zemindars of the plains encouraged their predatory habits by employing them against each other. They accordingly lived by rapine; and not only was the neighbourhood of the hills and the roads traversing them unsafe, but so was the passing of boats by the Ganges. This continued to be the case even for a long time after the establishment of the English power; and the Government dák-runners were frequently murdered and their wallets plundered. Troops were

sent to chastise the offenders; but the jungles on
their hills were impervious, and there were no roads
besides stony and steep footpaths by which to come
up to them. The Mahomedans had encountered the
same difficulty in their day, and had left the hillmen
uninterfered with; but the English Government was
determined to subdue them, and eventually succeeded
in doing so by tact and kindness. This new policy
was introduced by two young Captains of the East
India Company's army, named Brooke and Brown,
who invited and feasted the hill-chiefs and their
dependents in their camps, and then sent them home
with presents of turbans, beads, and other similar
trifles. The act awakened a new feeling in their
minds, which was promptly availed of by Mr. Cleve-
land, a young civilian, who was then the judge and
magistrate of Bhaugulpore. He visited the savages
in their own hills, unarmed and almost alone,
distributing presents to and feasting hundreds of
them at a time; and they were by these means
induced, first, to come to a parley, and, eventually, to
a definite understanding with the Government, which
has always been respected by them. There were
some disputes afterwards between them and the
zemindárs at the foot of the hills, in respect to
boundaries and the rights of wood and grazing;
upon which the hill-territory was, in 1832, separated
from the plains, demarcated, and, with every right
re-acquired from the zemindárs, made over to the

hillmen rent-free, on the sole condition of good
behaviour, which they have faithfully observed. Even
the Sonthals are no longer interfered with by them,
so long as they do not attempt to ascend their hills,
the two races occupying their respective allotments
seemingly without any knowledge of each other.

The Páháriáhs are shorter in size even than the
Sonthals, and also of slighter make; but their frames
are well knit and their limbs finely turned; and they
have always been very adventurous and brave. They
are of a fair complexion, and have broad faces, small
eyes, and flattish, up-turned noses; and their women
are pretty, and have good figures. The men are
very fond of dandyism, and oil and comb their hair
carefully, and tie it up in a knot on the head, passing
two long locks over the ears. Over the knot a red
turban is sometimes worn, their only other clothing
being a *dhoti* worn round the loins. The women are
dressed in skirts of white, and have each a square of
gay-coloured tusser silk which is passed over the
right shoulder and under the left, and tucked under
the skirt at the waist. They also wear coral necklaces, but no metal ornaments beyond rings and
chains. The principal tribal divisions of the race
are three—namely, the Malers, Máls, and Kumárs; of
whom the first retain more of the habits of their
ancestors than the other two. The Malers occupy
the heights of the Dámun, while the heights of
the southern or Rámgurh hills are occupied by the

Máls and the Kumárs, who differ from the Malers in
several essential respects, through having fraternised
largely with other races. The Máls, for instance, are
very fond of dancing, like the Koles and the Sontháls,
and of social enjoyments generally; but the Malers
are of a less cheerful disposition and never dance.
The former, again, are more particular in the matter
of food, having so far picked up Hindu prejudices
that they will not eat beef, nor any food not cooked
by themselves; but the latter are bound by no such
restrictions, and eat anything that they can procure.
The staple food of all tribes consists of maize, *janerá*,
and beans, which are mainly raised on the table-land
and slopes of their hills; but every other necessary of
life has to be obtained by them from the plains, by
bartering their bamboos, grass, and timber, all of
which grow in great profusion on the hills. The
crops are all raised by the women, and the process of
cultivation is of the simplest kind, the only instrument
used being an iron-shod staff, or pointed stick, with
which holes are made on the hill-side, at a distance of
a foot from each other, into which a mixture of seeds
is thrown—namely, of the crops intended to be raised.
The men are industrious after their own manner:
they will submit to any privations to have a shot at a
deer, or to secure a peacock; roam over the forests
for many miles in search of honeycombs, wild yams,
and gums; manufacture their bedsteads and sowing
staffs; bring down to the plains for sale wood,

charcoal, bamboos, cotton, and honey ; but they will
not stoop to clear the hill-side, or to cultivate. Here
the women intervene, and offer assistance loyally :
" I will do what you won't," says the wife to her lord ;
and who can help loving such a wife ?

The villages of the Páháriáhs have generally a
rather civilised appearance, being surrounded by
gardens and cultivation-patches. Though they are
very dirty in person themselves, their houses and
grounds are always kept free from filth and bad
smells. The huts are all carefully built of wattled
bamboos, no mud whatever being used in their
construction; and there are always numerous out-
houses for holding grain, pigs, etc. As among several
other of the wild races we have noticed, the unmarried
adults of both sexes are excluded from the family
residence, the males clubbing together to occupy a
bachelors' hall, while the females are put into distinct
cells provided for them. The intercourse between the
sexes, however, is not much restricted, and the lads
and lasses are always to be seen romping and love-
making, every facility being given to them to do so,
for the race is naturally amorous, though the lovers
do not necessarily misbehave. The fear of being
outcasted is very great, since no one can be re-
admitted into society till after expensive sacrifices ;
and this keeps things straight till the marriage knot
is tied. The process followed in getting united is
very simple. After selection has been made and

approved, the bridegroom goes for the bride to her
father's house ; and, as soon as the father has joined
their hands together, the young man marks the head
of the girl with *sindoor* with his right-hand little
finger, and then, linking the same finger with the
little finger of her right hand, leads her out of the
house to his own, while all the party entreat him to
be kind and loving to her. One of the most significant
admonitions to him on the occasion is that he must
not murder her, and this is accompanied by an
explanatory note that if she dies a natural death,
or by means of the devil, he would not be held
responsible for it. Polygamy is allowed and practised,
the value of female labour being great; and usually
one man has no less than four wives. Widow-marriage
is also permitted, and when a man dies his brothers
marry up all the widows, as they cannot afford to let
them go out of the family. The dead are buried.
The religion of the Páháriáhs recognises a Supreme
Being, who is named Budo Gossáin, and is represented
by the Sun, with other gods under him, each village
having a tutelary deity of its own. The Supreme
God created seven brothers, they say, to possess the
earth ; and they pretend to be descended from the
eldest of them. Their belief in evil spirits is so great
that a long bamboo is fixed in the ground in front of
every house to ward off their influence. The belief
in the transmigration of souls and in a future state is
also general. One peculiar custom of theirs is for

the priest to declare truths respecting the future by
an interpretation of his own dreams. He affects to
be inspired by fits of madness, when he lives apart
from all others in the depths of forests and jungles,
and receives, or manufactures, the dreams he inter-
prets. This curious imposition apart, the Páháríáhs
never deceive or lie. Oaths are taken on the arrow,
or on two arrows fixed on the ground with a little
salt placed between them, and never are such engagements violated. Their one great sin is drunkenness,
the beverage in general use being the *pachudi*, the
same that is so well loved by the Sonthals. In all
other respects they have been much reclaimed from
the barbarism that belonged to them at one time, and
are now usefully employed in several capacities; but
it is believed that they are declining in vigour, and
gradually dying out.

MINOR TRIBES IN BENGAL.

Apart from the races named above, there are several
minor tribes located in the wilds between Bengal and
Behár, and between Bengal and Cuttack, and also
to the west of Chotá Nágpore, the population of
which places is almost wholly aboriginal. The reason
why more such races are found in these localities
than in any other part of India seems to be that
they were driven to them as to an extremity by the
successive tides of conquerors by whom they were

pursued, there being no securer spot to fly to, since
these are all quite impervious for military operations.
Besides the races already spoken of and their sub-
divisions, we accordingly find here: the Bhárs, the
Cheroos, the Kanjhars, the Náts, the Thároos, the
Kárwárs, the Puttooás, and the Sours, of whom the
first and the second are not tribes of sufficient
importance or number at present to require further
notice here, the bulk of both having intermingled
with the more powerful communities about them,
while the third and the fourth are cognate tribes of
the vagabond race, best known as the gipsies, who
will be referred to hereafter in connexion with the
wild tribes of the south, as also will be the Thároos
along with the frontier races occupying the Terái,
where they reside in greater numbers.

THE KÁRWÁRS.

Of the rest, the principal seat of the Kárwárs is
Sirgoojá, whence they extend in one direction to
Palámow, and in another to Rewáh, while to the direct
north they approach the borders of Mirzápore and
Benáres. They are a dark, savage-looking people,
strongly-built and active, but short-legged; better-
looking, however, than the Oráons and the Gonds.
Though more hirsute than their cognates they never
cultivate their hair or beards, which gives to their
coarse features a wilder expression. They live in
detached hamlets rather than in villages, for even

among themselves they cannot agree to live together except in very small clusters. Their women are excessively hard-worked, and are stunted in growth, black, ugly, and wretchedly clad, having all the burdens of life imposed on them without any of the privileges belonging to their sex. The men may be idling all day, but the women must cultivate and work, hew wood and bring water. They always cultivate newly cleared ground, and for that purpose change their homestead every two or three years. The crops grown are rice, millet, yams, chillies, pumpkins, cucumbers, and arrowroot; but the yield is not very considerable in any case. They are put to no straits, however, on that account, for they have as sure a knowledge of what is edible among the jungle-produce as the monkey; and, on failure of their usual food-supply, easily find out something else to live upon. They know how to smelt iron, and trade in it, and also in honey, beeswax, resins, gums, and sticklac. They do not know aught of Sing Bongá or any other god, and worship nothing, but they sacrifice to their ancestors. One sept of them, the Khurriáh Kárwárs, have been partially Hinduised, and occasionally worship an idol named Khurriáh Ráni, a bloodthirsty goddess like Káli, to whom buffaloes in large numbers are sacrificed. Another sept are the Bhogtáhs, who are prominently distinguished as being more lazy and unimprovable than all the rest.

THE PUTTOOÁS.

The Puttooás, or Mangás, are scattered over the
Tributary Mehals of Cuttack, particularly over
Keonjhur, Pál Leyrá, and Dhenkenál. Their forms
are slight, and their physique seemingly weak. The
men are far from being handsome, while the women
are decidedly ugly, being a shade more frightful
even than those of the Kárwárs. The dress of the
men ordinarily is that of the Ooryáh peasantry
about them; but the women wear no clothes, their
sole covering being two large bunches of leaves, of
which one is worn in front and the other behind,
both being kept in position by a string of beads
passed twenty or thirty times round the loins. It
is from this original costume that the tribe has
acquired the name of *Puttooá*, or the leaf tribe.
They have no covering for the upper part of the
person, but the females wear necklaces of different
colours which hang down to their waists. For the
origin of their sylvan attire they have different
legends, which agree in representing it as a punishment inflicted on them by a *Rishi*, or by Devi
herself, for their pride in having been originally
much given to fine clothes! And the penalty of
abandoning the dress imposed on them is, they
believe, that they would be eaten up by tigers.
Within the last few years a supply of clothing has,
from time to time, been distributed among them by

the Government, and they have consented to wear
it; or at least the men have come to an engagement
to that effect on behalf of their women. They
are equally rude in other respects, and neither own
lands nor cultivate, though they are not undisposed
to assist others in cultivating. Their principal
pursuit is the chase, and they use their bow and
arrows with dexterity, killing deer, hogs, and snakes.
They eat everything except the cow; but their
usual food consists of roots and seeds of jungle
grass. They affect to be Hindus; but no Hindu,
however low his caste may be, will agree to eat or
mix with them. Their religion consists of the
worship of nameless spirits that are believed to
inhabit their woods and mountains. Marriages
among them are arranged by parents, and give
occasion to much revelry and drunkenness, the
festivities continuing for three days. The ceremony
consists in the thumbs of the pair being tied
together by a thread, which typically expresses
their union through life.

THE SOURS.

The Sours are chiefly found in the jungles of
Khoordá, from Bánpoor to Cuttack, and in the
woods which skirt the hills some way to the north
of the Mahánadi. They are of very inferior stature
and mean appearance, and are jet black in colour;

but they are in general harmless and peaceable,
though entirely destitute of moral sense, being very
like wild men of the woods. Some of them live in
villages, which are called *sais*, and find employment
with the zemindárs in clearing jungles and bringing
fuel, besides which they also collect the produce of
their woods, which they sell in the neighbouring
bazárs. Others lead a purely migratory life, wandering from spot to spot, where they erect temporary
huts of sticks, leaves, and grass, and clear the ground
for raising the grains they live upon, for the year
only. They eat almost everything they can come at,
and many of them have often nothing better to
subsist upon than roots and jungle-berries. Their
one constant arm is the axe; but it is used only
in felling trees.

CHAPTER V.

TRIBES OF THE MADRÁS PRESIDENCY.

THE KHONDS.

THE Khonds are the principal aborigines of the Eastern Gháts, their country extending from the eastern limit of Gondwáná to the Bay of Bengal, and from the Mahánadí river on the north to the Godávery on the south. A great part of this territory is excessively hilly, and the central table-land has an elevation of about 2,000 feet above the sea. Some portions of the plateau are perfectly bare of wood, but others are covered with trees ; and at the foot of it are impenetrable bamboo forests, which grow closer and resist the axe better than every other species of vegetation. The Khond districts are situated both in the plateau and the forests, and belong mainly to the Madrás Presidency, though running also into the dependencies of both Bengal and the Central Provinces. The proper name of the country is *Khondestán;* but a large portion of it is subject to the zemindárs of Goomsur and Chinná Kimedy on one side, and of Boád and

Duspullá on another, the Khonds inhabiting the mountain ranges only, in nominal subjection to the zemindárs. Much was therefore not known of this people before the Goomsur Rebellion of 1836-37, when the British troops ascended the Gháts in pursuit of the Rájáh of Goomsur, who, failing in his feudatory obligations, had defied the paramount power and fled to the Khonds for protection. The Rájáh died shortly after, committing his family to the care of the Khonds; and the Khonds, refusing to give up their guests, became amenable to the penalties of rebellion. They were not unfriendly towards the British Government at the outset, but, being goaded on by the representations of the people of Goomsur, resolved subsequently to repel force by force, which led to a harassing and miserable war, in which they were shot down like wild beasts, and their villages laid in ashes. They were finally compelled to submit, at the same time that the widow and son of the Rájáh of Goomsur were captured; and the first war with them was thereby terminated. But fresh complications were developed within a few years after, or as soon as their strange social organisation came to be understood. The British Government was surprised to find that the wild inhabitants of the Gháts were in the habit of offering human sacrifices to their gods, and also of systematically destroying their female children. It insisted on both the customs being abandoned, and there was a fresh war on the Khonds refusing to comply. As on the first occasion, however, they soon found that it was useless to resist, and, seeing no other way of getting over the difficulty, made whatever promises were demanded of them. It is doubtful if either of the practices objected to has been altogether discontinued even now in the wilder parts of their country impervious to the influence of the Government. This at least is certain, that the humanity which ordered their abolition has not anywhere been appreciated. The Khonds were permitted, at their own request, to denounce the British Government to their gods as the real cause of their apostasy, and, as the gods made no objection to transfer their wrath in the direction indicated, the Khonds have accepted their falling off from the faith of their ancestors as an inevitable evil. But it cannot yet be said truly that they have got reconciled to the change.

The Khonds are a wilder race even than the Gonds and the Bheels as they are now to be seen, and have as yet resisted all efforts made to civilise them. The men are well formed, of a good height, good-looking, and remarkably active; but the women are short in stature and very plain. In colour they are all much fairer than the Gonds, but varying in hue from that of copper to yellowish olive. In the upper elevations both sexes, for the most part, go naked, and, when pinched by cold, alleviate its excess by

H

making fires, while, when the heat of the weather becomes oppressive, they seek shelter under the shade of large trees. The only covering worn by the men in the lower elevations is a coarse cloth wound round the loins, in such a manner as to make the end hang down behind as low as the flaps of a coat, while the head-dress is formed by the hair being rolled up like a horn and then covered with a piece of red cloth decorated with feathers. The lower dress of the women in the same places is nearly like that of the men, with the addition of a gayer fringe; but it rarely descends under the knee, and there is no covering whatever for the upper part of the body. The ornaments in use are brass rings worn on the ear by both sexes, and also on the nostrils by women; the latter likewise wearing necklaces, armbands, and anklets either of brass or of coloured beads. The arms of the men are a long staff, or, in lieu of it, an axe with the blade in two divisions, a sling, and the bow and arrows, the military dress also including a covering of leather or bear's skin for the breast, and a showy crest of cock's feathers on the head. All the Khonds are trained to the use of their weapons from their earliest years, and are especially dexterous in handling the sling and the axe. Like other wild tribes in general, they are constantly at feud, either among themselves or with their neighbours; and on these and similar occasions they march to battle in what they consider to be a very impressive manner, singing and shouting, and always under the influence of strong potations. The different tribes fight with each other on the merest trifle; but one of their remarkable customs is that, as soon as the fighting is terminated, the women pass over from both sides to condole with each other on the loss of their nearest and common relatives. The general peace occupation of the race is agriculture, which is followed with great skill and energy, the result being that they are surrounded by every form of rural affluence. Rice of several sorts, millet, pulses, oils, tobacco, turmeric, and mustard are all grown on the hills; and the surplus stores of them are exchanged with the Brinjáris, or at fairs, for salt, cloth, and brass utensils and ornaments. They have also large herds of buffaloes and cattle of small breed, numerous flocks of goats, and abundance of swine and poultry. Of handicraft they know almost nothing, and indeed affect to despise it; but their huts are nevertheless well made, and are superior to those of the people living below the Gháts. Their general knowledge is very inconsiderable, for they will not submit to learn anything. Even the Gonds, we have seen, have been partially humanised by their contact with the Brinjáris; but no similar result has yet been obtained among the Khonds. Till recently the value of money was not understood by them, and up to this day barter among them, as among the Gonds, is chiefly in kind. Their language, like that of the Gonds, is peculiar to themselves, and is not understood even by their nearest lowland neighbours. Among the agreeable features in their character are: their love of independence, bravery, hospitality, and industry; while the qualifying traits of it include vindictiveness, ferocity, and inordinate debauch.

The primary divisions or classes among the Khonds are three—namely, the Maliáhs, or highlanders, who were originally independent of the zemindárs, and to this day pay no tribute to them; the Benniáhs, who occupy the outskirts of the hills and pay rents for the lands they hold, or account for it by service at their choice; and the Bhetiáhs, a servile class who hold lands on the condition of labour only. The administrative arrangements among all of them are the same, and indeed are based on local divisions of villages and districts, the chiefs, who are always selected for their deeds of valour, being of two sorts—namely, the village chiefs, whose jurisdiction is limited, and the district or superior chiefs, who exercise greater powers. The village chief in Chinná Kimedy is called Mánjee; in Goomsur, Mulliko; and in Boád, Khonro; while the district chiefs are called Bissoees in some places, and Páthurs in others. There is another officer in every village, named Digáloo, or minister, the best spokesman among the villagers being always selected for the post; and it is his duty to regulate the public meetings and assemblies of the people. These

meetings are purely democratic, and even women
are allowed to attend them, though they are not
permitted to take part in the discussions except
among particular classes. As a rule the women are
not trusted with any affair of importance till it
has been separately sat upon. " They *may* betray
counsel," say the Khonds, "though the youngest
stripling who can bear an axe will never blab of
what has been confided to him." For the head
of a family all the tribes have the greatest respect,
it being a proverb with them that " A man's father
is his God on earth." The social organisation
among them is indeed strictly patriarchal, the father
of a family being its absolute ruler in every case.
Disobedience to him under any circumstances is
regarded as a crime, and, even when the children are
separately lodged, the board is one, for no Khond
will ever venture to mess apart from his parents.
In their dealings with each other they are usually
very faithful, but only within tribal limits. Beyond
those limits they are almost as much robbers and
spoilers to each other as to strangers. No man can
approach a Khond village without being invited to
enter it; but, once in, he becomes a guest, and cannot
be turned out, and the murderer is safe even among the
children of the murdered. The ordinary food of the
Khond is *Khichree*, or rice and *dál* boiled together;
but the hunters eat freely of game. They draw no
milk from their domestic animals, but eat flesh of

all kinds, except of dogs, cats, and beasts of prey. Their love of liquor and tobacco is excessive, and the cultivation of tobacco among them occupies a large area. The liquors drunk are of different kinds— namely, those distilled from rice, the *mohowd* flower, and the fruit of the *áppá* tree respectively. A palm peculiar to their country also yields toddy, which is pleasant when fresh, but exceedingly intoxicating in a fermented state. They are fond, too, of dancing, and there is a place set apart for this amusement in every village. The dance is accompanied by music, and the performers are of both sexes. The men have a separate war dance, when they are armed to the teeth and lavishly decorated with red cloth and feathers; and also another dance, which represents a bison-hunt. On both these occasions the battle-axe is brandished as an accompaniment to the dancing, while in the other dances generally the only accompaniment is that of the pipe.

The appearance of a Khond village is rather picturesque, it being usually situated either by a clump of trees, or at the base of a wooded hill, or on the knoll of a valley. It consists of some forty or fifty houses, all built on one uniform model, like the cells of a beehive, the patrician and the plebeian being lodged precisely alike. The number of apartments in each house is three, of which the central room is the family dwelling-place, while the other two rooms are appropriated as a cooking-room and store-room respectively. The bachelors of the village, as among the Gonds, Sonthāls, and Páháriáhs, have a separate house assigned to them; and the maidens also, as with the Oráons, have their distinct quarters, though chastity is not a Khond virtue, and the separation of the young people is not very strictly enforced. All the Khond tribes intermarry; but, reversing the usage prevailing in other places throughout India, boys of ten and twelve are married to girls of fifteen and sixteen. The marriage arrangements are completed by the parents of the parties to be united, and generally in the following fashion :—The father of the bridegroom pays from twenty to thirty head of cattle to the father of the bride as the price of his daughter-in-law, engaging that her chief duty would be to act as a domestic servant in his house. A quantity of rice and liquor are then brought forward, and a libation is poured out to the gods, after which the high contracting parties join hands and declare the contract completed. A feast and a drinking bout follow, in the midst of which the bride is carried off, either on the back of the bridegroom, if he be up to her weight, or by some other person acting on his behalf, to give the affair the semblance of abduction, while all the young women of the bride's party follow the ravisher, and pelt at and abuse him, till he gains the bridegroom's house, when his assailants return home laughing and jubilant. Concubinage is not

considered dishonourable by the Khonds, and an
unmarried woman is not disgraced by becoming a
mother; though, of course, people are not over
anxious to marry her. Women have also the right
to quit their husbands at pleasure; and this right is
availed of among all the tribes—among some as
many as eight or ten times. The parents on such
occasions have to return the prices that were paid
for their daughters, and the trouble and vexation
this gives rise to causes a married daughter to be
regarded as a curse. The dead among the Khonds
are burnt, but without any rite or ceremony, except
that the burning of the body of a chief is accompanied
by the beating of drums and gongs.

The religion of the Khonds consists of the worship
of the Sun and the Earth, the former under the name
of Burá Pennu, or Belá Pennu, and the latter under
the name of Tárá Pennu. There are six or seven
subordinate deities besides—namely, of rain, spring,
wealth, the chase, war, boundaries, and judgment;
while a third class of gods comprises the descendants
of human beings who resisted evil in life, and are
believed to preside over villages, hills, streams,
fountains, tanks, houses, and forests. The Meriáh
sacrifices in Goomsur and Boád were to the Earth-
goddess alone, under the effigy of a peacock, and
were made under the belief that the process of
fertilisation could only be facilitated by drenching
the sterile soil with blood. Elsewhere the sacrifice

was to a number of deities, of whom the most
important were the Sun God and the God of War ;
and in some few places, again, no sacrifice whatever
was made, the people regarding such practices with
horror. The victims, where sacrified, were in some
places of both sexes, in others males only. They
might be of any caste or parentage, provided they
were not Khonds, for it was contrary to rule to
sacrifice a Khond. Foreign children were accordingly
purchased and brought up for sacrifice ; and they
were always kindly treated till they became of age
to understand what they were destined for, from
which time they were kept guarded and fettered.
The *Zanee*, or priest, officiated at the sacrifice, but
performed *poojah* to the idol through the medium of
the *Toombd*, a Khond child under seven years of
age. For a month prior to the sacrifice there was
much feasting and intoxication, with dancing round
the Meriâh, or victim, who was adorned with garlands,
etc. ; and on the day before the rite he was stupefied
with toddy and bound at the bottom of a post. The
assembled multitude then danced round the post to
music, singing hymns of invocation to some such
effect as follows:—" O God, we offer a sacrifice to
you ! Give us good crops in return, good seasons,
and health." On the next day the victim was again
intoxicated, and anointed with oil, which was wiped
from his body by those present, and put on their own
heads as a blessing The victim was then carried

in procession round the village, preceded by music, and on returning to the post a hog was sacrificed to Zakári Pennu, or the village deity, usually represented by three stones, the blood from the carcass being allowed to flow into a pit prepared to receive it. The victim, made senseless by intoxication, was now thrown into the pit, and his face was pressed down till he died from suffocation in the blood and mire, a deafening noise with instruments being kept up all the time. The Zanee then cut a piece of flesh from the body and buried it with ceremony near the village idol, all the rest of the people present going through the same form after him, while bits of flesh were also interred in the village boundaries. The head and face of the victim were left untouched, and, with the bones when bare, were buried in the pit.

The other crime which was common among the Khonds—namely, the destruction of female children—was justified by them on the score of the difficulty they experienced in getting the children married. The Khonds entertain a low opinion of female morality, and their young men are not eager to take upon themselves the responsibilities of the married state. "How, then," asked the elders, "were the girls under such circumstances to be supported?" Then, again, much vexation was caused to parents by the frequent disruptions of the marriage tie, which necessitated the return of the prices paid for the girls at the time of the marriage; and the best way of obviating such perplexities, it was thought, was to do away with the girls in their infancy. In some places, such as the remoter hills of Chinná Kimedy, male offspring were also killed, but only when the priest or astrologer discovered that the life of the child foreboded evil either to its parents or to the village. In all cases the method of destruction was identical. The infant was placed in a new earthen vessel, the mouth of which was closed, and which was then buried, after being marked with streaks of black and red. Both the Meriáh sacrifice and infanticide have now been tabooed for nearly forty years, and are believed to have been generally abandoned; but all parts of the Khond country have not yet been fully explored, and the news from the wilder corners scarcely come to civilised ears. In some places schools have been set up for the education of Khond children, but it will be a long time yet before these are able to humanise the people to any appreciable extent.

THE SAURÁS.

The Deccan, which includes all the countries to the south of the Nermuddá, was, at one time, the principal seat of the aboriginal tribes—at least, down to the banks of the Godávery. The number of them that burrowed in the caves of its mountains or roamed through its pathless forests was very

great, and contributed most to strengthen the Mahrattá and Pindári ranks, in which many of the races
were finally absorbed. The remnants that did not
disappear in this way still exist; but they are now
disjointed and scattered, and, apart from the Gonds,
Bheels, and Khonds, and the small migratory tribes
of the Central Provinces whom we have noticed,
those requiring to be especially mentioned are not
many, the most prominent among them being the
Saurás, the nearest neighbours of the Khonds to
the south, who extend from Chinná Kimedy to the
Godávery, or over a region nearly two hundred
miles in length, which is almost entirely unexplored.
If the Khonds are better looking than the Gonds,
the Saurás are, almost to an equal extent, better
looking than the Khonds. They are fairer in colour
and more athletic in appearance; and their habits
too are less dissipated, and their life in general less
turbulent. But, when this has been said, everything
that can be said in their favour is summed up.
They are fiercer than the Khonds, and so entirely
destitute of moral sense, that they will unhesitatingly
commit the greatest crimes for the paltriest advantages; and even the Khonds are so afraid of them
that, though always ready to fight among themselves, they are never anxious to provoke a quarrel
with the Saurás. The arms of the two tribes are
the same—namely, the battle-axe, and the bow and
arrows—and the Saurás are very apt in their use;

but they never attack their enemies except under cover of darkness, not being straightforward in any of their dealings. Even as thieves and plunderers, they always take every unfair advantage of their victims they can, without exercising their courage, though there is no question that they are quite as courageous as any other tribe.

MINOR TRIBES OF THE MADRÁS PRESIDENCY.

For the other races in the Deccan, we have to seek beyond the Godávery. The best part of the Eastern Gháts lies between the Kristná and the Cáuvery rivers, while the Western Gháts, which are higher and of uniform height throughout their entire length, run up from Cape Comorin to the Táptee river, coalescing with the Eastern Gháts between the districts of Coimbatoor and Malábár, where they form together the plateau or nucleus known as the Neilgherry hills. All the wild tribes that still exist in Southern India, exclusive of the Khonds and the Saurás, are crowded in and about this spot; but they are altogether very poor in number, and would scarcely be missed if no mention were made of them.

THE TODÁS.

The upper part of the Neilgherry plateau is inhabited by a wild tribe called the Todás, who

are fairer even than the Saurás, from which it has
been inferred that they are not aborigines, but came
probably as conquerors or immigrants from the sea.
They have received much attention mainly from
this belief, being too petty in numbers to be noticed
on any other account. The subdivisions of the tribe
are named: the Peikee, Kenná, Pekkan, Kuttan, and
Todi, of which the first is by far the most important.
The men are all well-made and above the common
height, and have a bold bearing, and open, expressive countenances. Their eyes are large, the nose
Roman, and the face always good-humoured. The
dress worn by them consists of a short under-garment
folded round the waist and fastened to a girdle, and
a *chádur*, or mantle, which covers the upper part of
the body except the head and the right arm. There
is no covering for the head in any weather, and
they allow the hair to grow to the length of six
or seven inches, parting it from the centre or crown,
and wearing it in bushy circlets dangling around.
No weapons whatever are carried by them beyond a
rod or wand, which helps them in the management
of their herds. The women have a modest and
retiring demeanour, but are not timid. They have
beautiful long tresses, which flow in unrestrained
luxuriance over neck and shoulders. Their dress is
composed, as that of the men, of an upper and under-
garment, but differently worn, the upper garment
enveloping the whole frame except the head, which

remains uncovered. The ornaments used are necklaces of twisted hair or black thread, with metallic
clasps, and, here and there, a knot from which are
suspended cowry shells; armlets and bracelets of
metal; and a sort of metal chainwork round the
waist. Both the men and women are equally dirty;
and the hamlets they dwell in, which are called
morts, and are composed of thatched huts resembling
the tilt of a wagon in appearance, are so offensive
within that they cannot be entered. The occupation
of the race is very peaceful—namely, tending herds
of buffaloes only. They do not keep poultry, pigs,
sheep, or goats; and even cows are not considered
worth bringing up. Their buffaloes are of a much
superior breed to those of the low country
generally, and the milk they yield is very rich.
Their repast is accordingly composed of milk, meal,
parched grain, and butter, no luxuries of any sort
being cared for; and even the use of salt is unknown
to them. The only articles they deal in are butter
and *ghee*, which they dispose of in the plains. Their
religion is as peaceful as their habits. Their god is
represented by a rude stone, to which *ghee* and milk
are given, but not blood in any shape. There are
priests among them who are bound to lead a life
of celibacy, those married before ordination being
obliged to live separate from their wives, so that
they might divest themselves of all worldly thoughts
and wishes, and dedicate their whole time to the

contemplation of the Deity. All this represents the
race as being inoffensive, virtuous, and happy. But
there is another side of the picture to look at.
Though endowed with great physical strength and
capacity to endure fatigue, they have no agricultural
industry to occupy them—no active employment of
any kind ; and, being indolent and slothful, are not
strangers to the passions and vices those habits call
forth. The priests in particular lead a very loose
life; and cases of plurality of husbands and lovers
among the women are frequent.

THE ERILIGÁRU.

Another wild people inhabiting the same plateau
are the Eriligáru, who also extend for a short distance
into the forests lying at the foot of the hills. They
are utterly unskilled in the arts of life, go nearly
naked, sleep under trees, and believe themselves to be
able to charm tigers. It is said of their women that
when they go into the wood in search of food they
intrust their children to the tigers, and receive them
back, safe and sound, on their return! Their villages
are called *cambays*, and are posted on the mountain
sides, around a square enclosure in which a large fire
is maintained at night to keep them warm and drive
away wild beasts from them. They breed goats and
cows, catch wild fowls in nets, and tigers in traps, and
have large orchards of plantain and lime trees. The

language spoken by them is a jargon compounded of the dialects of the different races in their vicinity, by contact with whom they are gradually getting humanised.

THE KÁRUBÁRUS, ETC.

Near the foot of the hills dwell also the Kárubárus, Kurumbárs, and Kohátees, all small, scattered, and harmless races, and the first two of the same character precisely as the Eriligáru—that is, equally unskilled in the arts of life. The occupation these chiefly follow is that of hired labourers to watch the fields against the depredations of birds and wild hogs; but the third, unlike them, are able to cultivate, and also make themselves useful in the hills as smiths, potters, and artisans of every description.

THE SOLIGÁS.

Another wild people, named the Soligás, inhabit the hills in the vicinity of the Cáuvery, and are known as being remarkably rude, and having features not unlike those of the savages of Chittagong, which suggests a possible descent from naval immigrants from across the bay. The huts they build are so wretched that they can hardly live in them, and use them rather as store-rooms and cooking-sheds, sleeping in the open air at night around a fire, with plantain-leaves used both as mattresses and coverings. By day they go nearly naked, but are so busily employed in the depths of the forests that they

I

are rarely seen. They search the forests for lac, beeswax, honey, yams, and esculent leaves; and also hew timber for sale. They keep no domestic animals, nor know the art of killing game; but are not wholly ignorant of agriculture, of which the principal labour devolves on their women. Polygamy is permitted among them, adultery unknown; and the aged are well cared for by their children and relatives.

THE NIADIS.

The Niadis are another tribe belonging to the same locality. They are very like the Soligás in their habits, living nearly naked, and wandering about in unfrequented places in search of what their woods will yield them. The huts they live in are as miserable as those of the Soligás, and are built under trees, in remote corners. Their principal occupations are to protect the crops from the depredations of wild hogs and birds; to rouse game for hunters; and to catch tortoises and crocodiles, which are eaten with avidity. Marriage, as a ceremony, is unknown among them; but one man lives with one woman only, and infidelity is scarce. Those of them who are shepherds live almost entirely with their flocks, the men sleeping in the open air, wrapping themselves in blankets, while the women and children are sheltered within temporary huts made of blankets, twigs, and leaves. Of their religion all that is known is that they sacrifice to a female spirit yearly.

THE GIPSIES.

The remaining wild tribes of South Deccan may be included under the general head of Gipsies, who are to be seen in every part of India, absorbing all classes of men of the lowest social grades. The race is so well known all over the world, and its counterparts are so like each other in every place, that no lengthened description of it is necessary. As a rule the men are tall, fine-limbed, and bony, but far darker in India than anywhere else; while the women have pretty though sunburnt faces, large, black, and brilliant eyes, and long hair. In some parts of India this people are called Bedyás, in others Náts, in others again Kanjhars and Bájikars, leading the same vagabond life everywhere. Some of them profess Hinduism, others are avowedly Mahomedans; but the main religion of all, the one common bond that binds them together, is thieving, which children weaned from the breast are taught with assiduity. Another common bond between the several septs is a secret language of their own—besides that they ordinarily use—which, it is said, is understood by Gipsies only, and all over the world. Their habits are entirely migratory; but they live in bands, and erect temporary huts wherever they encamp, from which they go about—men and women—as jugglers, strolling players, cattle-gelders, tumblers, and dancing-girls—doing every work in fact except what demands

I 2

labour and steadiness. Many of the men obtain a
living by leading about dancing-bears and monkeys;
many more, by catching birds, squirrels, and
mungooses; while among the women are those who
practise physic, fortune-telling, and tattooing. The
men are always as fantastically dressed as they can
manage; but the women have frequently nothing
beyond a ragged cloth round the waist, which is
usually coloured, while the children go naked. In
all parts of the world they are represented as eating
any kind of food they can come at; and in India
they are so uncleanly that they will eat even bullocks
and horses that have died of disease. Before marriage
there is no constraint on their passions; but after
marriage the wife· at least is generally faithful.
When the parties concerned have agreed to be united
the lover proceeds to the hut of his mistress to wed
her. Her relations thereupon meet him with a
mock refusal, but relent ·when they find him very
pertinacious, and, in giving up the girl, ask him to
behave kindly to her. Her forehead is marked by
him with *sindoor*, an observance appertaining rather
to the country than to the race; and this, completing
the ceremony, is followed by a banquet, in which
there is as much intoxication as the parties can afford
to pay for.

PART II.
THE FRONTIER TRIBES.

CHAPTER I.

TRIBES ON THE NORTH-WESTERN FRONTIER.

IN the preceding pages we have described all the more important internal wild tribes of India, aboriginal or otherwise. It remains now to notice the half-savage frontier tribes, who are for the most part not aborigines of the soil, though they have, from their long residence at the places into which they intruded, become semi-Indianised. On the North-Western frontier the chief of these tribes are: the Beloochees, Patháns, Wuzeerás, Bunnoochees, Murwátees, Áfreedees, Momunds, and Swátees, all of whom are divided into independent and dependent clans—namely, those occupying the outer face of the frontier, and those occupying its inner side as subjects of the British Government, respectively.

THE BELOOCHEES.

The Beloochees, the southernmost of the races named, are of tall and wiry make, and a rather dark

colour, with features decidedly Jewish, but marked
by an almost ferocious expression. They are divided
into several tribes or clans, of whom the most
important are: the Kusránis, Bozdárs, Khutráns,
Kosáhs, Singháris, Lisháris, Boogtis, Ghoorchánis,
and Madáris, the last two being the most warlike
and troublesome. The general character of the
entire race is marked by great vindictiveness,
treachery, and cruelty, and by a readiness at all
times to take offence at the merest trifle; but, on
the other hand, they are very hospitable—particularly
to the wayfarer and the stranger—free from religious
bigotry and fanaticism, and far more truthful when
trusted than many of the other races in their
neighbourhood. The Khán of Khelát is their
nominal sovereign: we say *nominal*, because they
are as often found ready to resist as to obey him.
They are a mercenary people, who would by nature
prefer to act as soldiers, but turn camel-drivers,
robbers, and cut-throats as willingly on the price
for such service being paid to them. They are
passionately fond of field-sports, but are otherwise
exceedingly indolent; and they abhor reading and
writing as effeminate and contemptible accomplishments. What they are now most famous for is their
breed of horses, which, though sorry-looking and
insignificant, are well adapted for the life led by
their owners, being swift of pace and so inured to
labour that they weary out the best racers in pursuit.

The arms of all the tribes are the same—namely, the matchlock, sword, and shield, and their fighting power taken together is not inconsiderable; but they are always at war with each other, and can never heartily combine for any common enterprise. Spirituous liquors are inordinately used by them, and the smoking of *bhang* is incessant, the pipe being in the mouth of both sexes, and at all times. The influence exercised over them by their women is great, it being commonly asserted that, though no confidence can be placed on engagements entered into by the men even when sworn to on the *Korán*, they will never depart from any agreement or stipulation to which their women are parties.

THE PÁTHÁNS.

The Páthán tribes lying to the north of the Beloochees are of stouter appearance, and, in fact, in physical development count among the finest races of the earth; and the height of pride on the border is to be recognised as a Páthán—that is, of Afghán descent. The race is very warlike, and in times past interfered frequently with the destinies of India; and many of the *kheyls* or tribes make fairly good soldiers to this day—such, for instance, as the Bungaish tribe who inhabit the Koház district, extending beyond the border into the Khoorum valley. All the men are rough and frank, but neither faithful nor trustworthy; fair to look at, though somewhat bronzed by the hot sun of India; and have no occupation but rapine, which can never be checked except by retaliation and reprisals. They are great fanatics also in religion; and, from one cause or another, have managed to keep their part of the frontier in turmoil at all times.

THE WUZEERÁS.

The Wuzeerás, who come next, hold the Goláree, Bolan, and Soorduk passes, and are a bold and ferocious people, though in soldierly qualities they are very far from being equal to the Pátháns. They are, however, as prone to plunder, and quite as careless of bloodshed, but are held to be comparatively less treacherous, as they will never entrap an enemy by false overtures. They are rather noble specimens of the savage character, and, though wholly without law, are not equally destitute of honour. The principal tribal divisions among them are: the Máhsuds, Áhmedzyes, Othmánzyes, and Bithunnees. The men are all stout and fierce-looking, and the women tall and stately. Their habits are nomadic, and they live usually under tents made of coarse blankets or reed mats, under which old and young huddle together for shelter, careless of the sun or rain. For subsistence they depend mainly on their flocks and herds, and in the winter months they are to be seen yearly moving with their camels, goats, and broad-tailed sheep towards the sheltered plains

of Bunnoo. Some of the tribes have also commenced
to cultivate. But they are never unready for bolder
and more hazardous undertakings, and the discharge
of a single matchlock will bring all the clans
together to act in concert, either as robbers or
soldiers; for, though enemies to all the world, they
have no disunion among themselves—which is, in
fact, their peculiar trait.

THE BUNNOOCHEES.

The Bunnoochees, or inhabitants of Bunnoo, are
a mongrel race descended from many races, and
differ from each other in stature, complexion, and
character. They may nevertheless be generally
described as being small in stature and having a
shrivelled appearance, along with all the vices of
human nature in their worst development. Less
cannot be said of them, indeed, than that they bring
discredit even on the Afghán name. Their family
dissensions are constant on account of their various
descent, and it is commonly remarked of them that
they are never at peace except when they are at
war. They acknowledge no king and hardly a
common chief, every *kheyl* having its separate
Mullik, or master, and being at enmity with all
others; but they acknowledge the Ákhoond of Swát
as their common high-priest, and are renowned for
their fanaticism. Their valley is fertile, and has an
abundant supply of water, and the crops grown by

them are various, including wheat, rice, sugar-cane, and turmeric. Cattle also are plentiful in it, and the people are necessarily rich in rural wealth of every kind.

THE MURWÁTEES.

The Murwátees are a fine manly race, neighbours of the Bunnoochees, but not like them either in appearance or character. They are a tall and muscular people, frank and simple in their manners, and conspicuous for their generous and manly treatment of their women. Their habits are both agreeable and pastoral, and while some of them are seen cultivating their lands, others are found wandering about with their flocks of goats and laden camels, or occupying temporary huts improvised wherever they encamp. The crops raised by those who cultivate are: wheat, barley, and grain; but their country is sandy, and much distress is felt for want of water, which lies so far below the surface that it is not easy to sink wells to get at it. It has therefore to be procured from distant springs; and a great portion of the time of their women is taken up by this work. Among themselves the people are very factious, their community being divided into two parties which are always quarrelling with each other.

THE ÁFREEDEES.

The Áfreedees have the reputation of being the most formidable of all the Trans-Indus tribes, and hold the principal passes leading into and out of India, along the hills lying between the Kabool river and the Khyber, which form the western boundary of the Peshawar valley. As soldiers they are among the best on the frontier, and every invader of India has had either to take them into his service or to pay for their neutrality. They are fierce by nature and exceedingly unmanageable and untrustworthy, but nevertheless always true to their salt. The main branches of the tribe are: the Ádum, Oolâh, Áká, Meerie, Karum, Bhyrám, and Orukzye *kheyls*, which are always at feud with each other when there is no common enemy to contend with. Their villages are all posted on the loftiest and most rugged hills, which enables them to defy even the hand of power with impunity; and they have accordingly never owned subjection either to the Kabool or to any other Government. In times of peace they are often employed as traders and carriers, and bring salt from the Kohát mines to the Peshawar market; but their innate ferocity inclines them most to deeds of blood. The Áfreedee mother prays that her son may be a successful robber; and the men are so faithless, that they will enter into engagements on the *Korán* after having already made up their minds to break them. They are armed at all times —even when only tilling the ground, or grazing cattle, or driving beasts of burden before them; and will use their weapons on the slightest provocation,

or to derive the smallest benefit. The only redeeming virtue in their character is their hospitality.
The guest, invited or uninvited, is always welcome
and safe; but, once fairly out of his entertainer's
door, must protect himself in the best way he can,
being no longer entitled to his forbearance.

THE MOMUNDS.

The Momunds are a powerful race, occupying the
Peshawar frontier from the left bank of the Kabool
river, opposite the Tárturrá Pass, to the right bank
of the Swát river in the neighbourhood of Abazie.
They live in very small hamlets generally, but have
a few large villages and towns; and are divided into
several tribes, of whom three are most important
—namely, the Tourkzyes, Báeezyes, and Khwáazyes.
The tribes best known to the British Government
are: the Pindee Áli, Álumzye, and Michnee *kheyls*,
whose raids and robberies on the frontier have been
incessant. They are all brought up as soldiers,
though our more recent knowledge of them in connexion with the just-concluded war in Afghánistán
has not altogether established their name for valour.
There is no question, however, that they are very
audacious as robbers, and, it is said, that they will
start up from their devotions, if informed of the
approach of a *káfiláh* of merchants, to plunder
them, and, after securing their booty, will return
to their prayers.

THE SWÁTEES.

The Swátees, the last race to be noticed, consist of various clans united under a loose federal government, with an elective chief, or king, at its head. They do not rank very high as warriors, but are as great plunderers as the rest, and did much outrage in the Peshawar plains in past times, regarding them as their natural hunting-grounds. They never attack any of the warlike races about them, but are savage in dealing with such cultivators, petty traders, and cattle-graziers as they may happen to meet with. Their ways and habits, however, are improving; and they have already begun to cultivate for themselves—namely, cotton, tobacco, and some kinds of pulses on their hills, and rice on their river banks. Their women have a great influence over them; but it is nevertheless said that they are frequently sold, or bartered for money, by their husbands.

All the tribes named above are wild and fierce, and most of them warlike also; and they have all the virtues and vices of the savage state in more or less degree, and often jumbled together in a confused and contradictory manner. Their common religion is Mahomedanism; but the creeds yet more generally understood by them are: "blood for blood" and "fire and sword for infidels." Retaliation and malicious persecution are, in fact, the strongest of

all obligations with them ; hospitality to all being at
the same time an obligation only next in degree.
They have no education to speak of, and are
superstitious and priest-ridden, their priests and
moollahs being as ignorant as themselves. This
makes them in some respects dependent on the
Hindu *Bunnidhs* living amongst them—the *Bunnidh*
on the frontier being something like the Jew as
the Jew is, and always has been, all over the world.
There is hardly any part even of Central Asia
where the *Bunnidh* is not seen. He is insulted
and tyrannised over wherever he goes, as the Jew
at one time was in Europe ; but the trade and
mercantile accounts of the whole country he lives
in are entirely in his hands, and this reconciles
him to the disadvantages of his lot. That lot is
very trying at times, for woe to the *Bunnidh* who
cannot hide his gold. The only protection against
the cupidity of the tribes he lives with is that to
be found in the *Zedruts*, or holy shrines, which are
always safe from spoliation, and travellers encamping
near which are generally unmolested : and this seems
to be a well-observed rule, not only on the north-
western frontier, but in all parts of south-western
Asia.

CHAPTER II.

TRIBES ON THE NORTHERN FRONTIER.

ON the northern frontier, the Himálayás, though rising almost suddenly in great height, are yet habitable for a considerable distance upland before the snows are reached; but almost all the accessible territory here, from Cashmere downwards, is mainly occupied by different Hindu races, till we come to the borders of Gurhwál and Kumáon.

THE BHOTEES.

The first of the wild tribes to be met with in this place are the Bhotes, or the Bhotees, a cross-breed probably between the Khásiáhs and the Huniás, who occupy the passes and even the centres and crests of the mountains between Buschár and Kumáon. Their appearance, manners, and peculiarities are very like those of the Khásiáhs, whom we shall presently describe, while their dialect is the same with that of Thibet. The habits of the race are nomadic, and they dwell chiefly in tents, almost entirely monopolising the trade across the mountains, which is carried, for the most part, on the back of their sheep. They also cultivate a little, principally in the Terái, where they always lodge during the winter months for *dhoopsekud*, as they call it—that is,.to bask in the sun—and where they graze their herds on the rich herbage with which they are overgrown.

THE KHÁSIÁHS.

The Khásiáhs are the immediate neighbours of the Bhotees, inhabiting the districts of Gurhwál and Kumáon, or all the mountain tract lying between the Alakánanda and the Káligungá. The race is an ancient one, enumerated in the *Institutes* of Menu under the name of Khásas, among the several Kshetriya races referred to by the legislator. They still claim to be of Rájpoot descent ; but even that would not make them aborigines of the country, the Rájpoots themselves being nothing more than Scythians. As now seen they exhibit clearly a mixture of Mongolian and Indian blood, though they have adopted the language and customs of the Hindus, and are anxious to be counted with them. They are strong in numbers, for they form about nine-tenths of the population of the provinces they inhabit, and extend from the foot of the mountains to the Terái, which separates them from Rohilkund. The men are of middle size, dark and meagre in

appearance, but well framed and active, and of
loftier stature than the Bhotees and other mountaineers in their neighbourhood. Their women have
handsome features, though they look sunburnt and
toil-worn. The dwelling of the race is chiefly under
tents, and the ordinary garment of the men is a
long black blanket, which is indispensable to them.
The dress of the women is a coarse cloth worn round
the waist, with the black blanket in addition passed
over the head and shoulders. The character of the
people being peaceable, no arms are carried by them
except sticks to drive away wild animals. The
women wear ornaments in the shape of metal anklets
and bracelets, and weighty rings in their ears and
noses. Polyandry prevails very widely among them,
and very frequently a family of brothers has only
one wife in common. Chastity and conjugal affection
hardly exist; but their attachment for children is
very strong. They are also sober and good-humoured,
and the women are very patient under privations.
The men being excessively indolent, the entire labour
of domestic economy and agriculture is left to the
women, with the exception of ploughing and harrow-
ing, which is performed by the men. It speaks much
to the credit of the women therefore, that, in every
part of their country where the declivity of their hills
will admit of the operations of a plough or spade,
small plots of ground are to be seen, all in a high
state of cultivation, and many of them ranged in

K

little terraces one above another, supported by walls
of loose stone. One portion of the race—namely,
those who do not live at any great distance from
the plains—migrate annually to the upper part of the
Terái during the cold weather, to "bask in the sun"
like the Bhotees, taking their cattle with them to
graze. They are always accompanied by their
families, and employ themselves in cultivating the
best and driest spots of the forest with barley and
wheat, which they reap and carry back with them,
returning again to gather their later crops, should
they have sown any. These opportunities are also
taken to dispose of their *ghee*, honey, and the produce
of their hills generally, in exchange for such luxuries
as are only to be obtained from the plains. They are
so honest that property amongst them is always left
exposed even when the owners are absent from home,
the use of lock and key being unknown. The only
precaution taken on such occasions is to fence their
grounds carefully with a view to keep out wild
animals from them.

THE BOKSÁS.

In the forests at the foot of the Sewálik hills live
the Boksás, who are as spare in habit as the
Khásiáhs, but shorter in stature, and are distinguished
by broad faces, depressed noses, thick lips, and very
scanty hair on the face. They are quite as simple
and inoffensive as the Khásiáhs, but, if possible, yet

more ignorant and unthrifty, and so very indolent
that they object to all labour which is not absolutely
necessary for subsistence. They have no arts or
manufactures among them; and the little clothing
they wear is imported. They cultivate to some
extent, but the produce is never abundant enough
to supply their wants fully. Their food is very
simple, consisting ordinarily of bread made of wheat,
barley, or millet, or of rice and *dál*, seasoned with
wild herbs cooked as greens; but their laziness is
so great that they are often, for want of these even,
compelled to subsist on yams and berries only.
Flesh in any quantity they cannot obtain, for, though
fond of deer and wild pigs, they will not take the
trouble to hunt for them, nor will they breed any
domestic animals, even fowls being but rarely reared
by them. The chief products of their forests are
bamboos and timber, which are cut for export. They
also collect drugs and gums for sale, and wash for
gold in the Soná Nadi and the Rámgungá, getting
in exchange for what they collect tobacco and
spirits, of both of which they are equally fond.
Their women, however, are not ordinarily allowed
to get drunk with them, for "what need have they
for spirits," say the men, "when they have neither
to go out into the jungles, nor to sit up whole nights
on a *máchán* watching crops?" One division of the
race lives to the east of the Rámgungá, where it is
concentrated, while the other dwells on the west of

the river, and is more loosely scattered. The Eastern Boksás show an invincible dislike to settle down on any particular spot for more than two years, though they never migrate outside of their forests or the Terái ; but the Western are not so restless, and many of them will never shift from their villages at all. There are some Boksá villages also in the Deyrá Dhoon, where the people are called Mehrás, though acknowledged by the other Boksás to be of the same caste with themselves. They all conform to the Hindu religion, though in an ignorant and unmeaning way, and in all small matters generally adhere to Hindu customs, as they understand them. The moral character of the race is excellent, and their good humour can only be compared with that of the Khásiáhs.

THE THÁROOS.

Side by side with the Boksás live the Thároos, who occupy all the Terái from eastern Rohilkund, along the frontiers of Oude, to Goruckpore and the Gunduck. The great mass of them are now subjects of the Nepál Government, having been transferred to it with the Oude Terái. They are very similar to the Boksás in several respects, but neither will acknowledge any relationship or connexion with the other. Both are apparently of Mongolian extraction, but seem to have intermixed largely with the Indian races, some of whom, such as the Koles, they

resemble to a considerable extent. The Thároos
are very shy and timid, but very frank and truthful,
and their women have a name for chastity. They
live in grass huts, and are less migratory than the
eastern Boksás, more nearly resembling the western
tribe in that respect. Their principal occupation is
cultivation, and their tillage is peculiar in this, that
it leaves large wastes between the patches that are
cultivated. Unlike the Boksás, they always raise
food-grains enough for their use, their women, who
are hardy, assisting them greatly in husbandry. They
are expert huntsmen also, and eat the game they
kill, as well as other flesh, not excluding that of
animals that have died of disease; and they drink
quite as largely as the Boksás, the habit having
perhaps been equally forced on both by their residence in the Teráí.

THE LIMBOOS.

The Limboos are found on the Nepál frontier, and
between Nepál and Sikkim, and form a numerous
tribe, which is said to have come originally from
the province of Chung in Thibet. They are scarcely
ever seen beyond the Teestá except as strangers;
but many of them have come and settled in and
about Darjeeling. Like the other hill-tribes near
them, they are short in stature, fair in complexion,
and completely beardless; but they are less fleshy
than some of them, as, for instance, the Lepchás.

The physical differences between the several races here located are, in fact, slender, and not obvious to strangers, and hence the usual practice of grouping them together. In former times, the Limboos were a warlike race; but they are now almost wholly given to agriculture, cattle-grazing, and petty trading. The two most important septs among them are named Hung and Rái. The habits and customs are the same with both, their dress consisting of wide trousers and a jacket, and their principal weapon being the kookri. They live in huts, which are very rudely made and inconvenient, a whole family having rarely more than one apartment. In religion they affect the Hinduism of Nepál, but in reality have gods and goddesses of their own, and one Supreme Deity over all. They do not build temples to any of these, nor make images of them; and their worship consists simply of offerings and sacrifices.

THE MURMIS.

The Murmis are also of Thibetan origin, and are found in all parts of the Nepál mountains, and in the Sikkim country, as far to the east as the Teestá. They are a numerous tribe in their original country, and as seen on the frontier are less changed in their habits than other races of similar descent. They are strongly made and active, and taller than the Limboos; but, though good-tempered, are not held to be of an equally cheerful disposition. Their habits are pastoral and agricultural, with this especial peculiarity in them, that they feed their sheep and goats on the highest elevations near the snows, and cultivate as great heights as are capable of producing maize and *murwá*. Their villages are accordingly perched on sites from 4000 to 6000 feet high, where they live in cottages built of stone and thatched with grass. Their religion is the Buddhism of Thibet. They are said to be very kind to strangers.

THE VÁYUS.

The Váyus, or Háyus, are another race dwelling on the confines of Nepál, on or about the tract where the Koosi enters India. They have a tradition among them of having at one time been a powerful people, but, as seen at present, are a very small race, verging gradually to extinction. Physically, they are of a medium height, brown colour, hazel eyes, and long black hair; and in character are at the same time inoffensive and industrious. They are employed chiefly in cultivation, and also in collecting the produce of their mountains.

THE KERÁNTIS.

A more powerful people in their neighbourhood are the Kerántis, who are said at one time to have held dominion down to the delta of the Ganges.

They are tall in stature and well-made, having a pale brown colour, well-formed face, large oval eyes, and straight jet-black hair. They are mostly subjects of Nepál, and in their own hills bear a fierce and quarrelsome character; but have a better name in Darjeeling, where they are much valued as servants, both menial and military service being now sought for by them to some extent. Their principal occupation on the hills is cultivation; and they raise crops of maize, buckwheat, millet, peas, rice, and cotton. They have no craftsmen among them, and are necessarily compelled to buy the implements, utensils, and ornaments they use. Their houses are built on hill slopes, being raised on the outer side on wooden posts to give them a level. The walls are of thick reeds plastered, and the roof of grass. Each family builds separately for itself, and children separate from their parents the moment they get married. The occupations of the women are spinning and weaving cotton of native growth, and thus all the clothes they wear are home-made. They also make the liquors—fermented and distilled—which they drink. Their usual way of obtaining a wife is either to buy her, or to earn her by labour in her father's family. Divorce can be had at the pleasure of either party; but, if the wife seek it, her family has to refund the price that was paid for her. Great veneration is paid by this people to their dead, whom they bury on the hill tops. They have no clear idea of religion, but two great religious festivals are held by them annually, one being in honour of Khyimmo, or the household deity, and the other in honour of the Sámkhá, or souls of the dead.

THE LEPCHÁS.

The Lepchás inhabit the southern face of the Himálayás, from the Tambár branch of the Koosi on the west, to the mountains of Bootán on the east, and are the subjects respectively of Nepál, Sikkim, and Bootán. They have been spoken of as the aborigines of the mountain forests surrounding Darjeeling; but there is less doubt that they are of Mongolian descent. The primary divisions of the race are two, named Rong and Khambá, of whom the former only profess to be indigenous, while the latter assert that they came originally from Khám, a province of China. They are both precisely alike in appearance, being short in size, but bulky for their height, and rather fleshy than sinewy. Their faces are broad and flat, nose depressed, eyes oblique; they have no beard at all, and a very little only of moustache. The complexion is olive, and may be called fair, and the children have even a ruddy tinge, which, however, is lost in adolescence. The total absence of beard, and the fashion of parting the hair along the crown of the head, gives the males an effeminate appearance, and, the robes of the two sexes being fashioned nearly alike, it is not always easy to distinguish them. The dress of the men consists of a cotton cloak, with a loose jacket also for those who can afford to have two, both bound round the waist; while the women have first a petticoat of cotton cloth, and over it something like a loose bedgown, fastened by a girdle. The hair is worn in long plaits by both sexes; but, while the men have a single pigtail, the women have two. The ornaments in use consist of necklaces of coloured beads and corals, and earrings; the women having, of course, more of both than the men. The arms of the men are the *kookri* and a long knife called *bán*, which they use nimbly in all work; besides which they have a bamboo bow and iron-pointed arrows. But they are not warriors, and use their weapons only against wild beasts and for cutting down forests; and they have their spade and hoe to help them in agriculture. They are not good cultivators, however, and, having no ploughs, only scrape the ground to put in the seeds, which does not yield them more food-grains than they require. The crops raised are: rice, wheat, barley, and millet; and, when the supply of these is very inadequate, they are obliged to subsist upon ferns, bamboo roots, and the innumerable succulent plants to be found in their mountains, besides which they eat all kinds of flesh, including beef and pork. Tea is a favourite beverage with them, and is brought from China; but they are even more fond of fermented and spirituous liquors, without however being given to excess. They make their beer themselves, and it is said to be refreshing; but the art of distillation is not known to them. In habits they are very dirty, and also excessively indolent, and, preferring to spend their time in hunting and loitering, they leave all out and indoor work to their women. They are perpetually moving about, and never remain in one place for more than three years, which is the period usually allowed by all nomad tribes for the freshness of the virgin soil to get exhausted. They have necessarily no permanent villages; but the huts they set up are, nevertheless, well made, being constructed entirely of bamboos, and thatched with the same material split up. Their cheerfulness of disposition is proverbial, and they are also honest—so much so, that theft is uncommon among them. Their good nature, too, is great, and though constantly wrestling and jumping, they are never seen to fight or quarrel with one another. In religion they are Buddhists, and are said to be somewhat superior to their neighbours, the Booteáhs, in morality. Chastity in adult girls previous to marriage is neither to be met with nor cared for; and the marriages are often allowed to take place on credit—that is, breakable if the payment bargained for is not made within the specified time; but girls married are usually faithful to their husbands.

THE BOOTEÁHS.

The Booteáhs are the inhabitants of Bobtán, where
they are independent; but they also occupy the
alpine regions adjacent to the British frontier, which
are known by the name of the Doárs, and are now
subject to the British Government. They can hardly
be counted among the *wild* tribes of India, for they
are, for the most part, in good circumstances, and
have a certain amount of civilisation among them;
though there is no doubt that, in some particular
respects, they are in worse plight even than the
worst savages we have described. The best account
we have of them is that given by Sir Ashley Eden,
who went to their country as an envoy in 1864. The
mission was unsuccessful, and led to the Bootán war,
by which the Doárs were acquired; but since then
the British frontier has been better respected than
it ever was before.

The Booteáhs are a short, square-built people,
with the true Kálmuck countenance—that is, having
a broad flat face, small and oblique eyes, a low and
short nose, and a large mouth, all shown to the best
advantage by a good-humoured expression, which
imparts attraction even to their physical defects.
The men are, for the most part, stout and ruddy,
and the women healthy-looking, if not handsome;
but they are both so excessively dirty that it is
never convenient to admire them except at a

distance. Their dress is the ordinary Tartar dress, consisting of large boots with trousers stuffed into them, caftàns girded round the waist, and little bonnets edged with black sheep's skin; the dress of the women varying to this extent, that they substitute a long cloak with loose sleeves for the coat worn by the men. Neither men nor women are much fond of indulging in ablutions, and their garments are never changed till they rot off; nor does it add to their attractions that the front of their coats is used as a pouch for holding everything, cooked rations included. Of one sect, the Dharmias, it is said that they never wash even their hands and faces except on particular occasions of religious ceremony, and use the skirts of their dress to cleanse alike their persons and cooking utensils. The ornaments most in fashion with all are large pins and amber beads; and corals are also worn by those who can afford to have them. The coarser clothes worn are woven by themselves, but the finer fabrics, whether of wool or silk, are imported from China and Thibet; and even a great portion of the food they live upon has to be procured from other places, as they are neither good agriculturalists nor good animal-breeders. The crops they raise are excessively scanty; and, though sheep and goats form the principal means of transport in their country, they have to be obtained from villages beyond the southern base of their mountains. Trade is therefore

an object of great importance to them, and they
hold in their hands a complete monopoly of the
carrying trade with Thibet. The articles supplied
to them from India are: grain of various kinds,
sugar, spices, tobacco, cotton cloths, and hardware;
while their imports to India consist of shawl wool,
woollen cloths, *chowries*, or tails of the yak or
mountain ox, and ponies. It is from this, their
principal occupation, that the modicum of civilisation they can boast of has been derived; and many
Booteáhs are able to read and write. Their houses,
also, are well built, and made of good materials,
though they are better looking from without than
convenient to live in. They make, too, the paper
they write upon, and have acquired knowledge of
distillation, which enables them to manufacture the
spirits they drink. But against these advances, so
far as they are such, has to be noted their extreme
laxity in morals, which it is not possible to exceed.
The marriage tie is so loose that chastity is quite
unknown amongst them. The husbands are indifferent to the honour of their wives, and the wives
do not care to preserve that which has no value
attached to it. Polyandry prevails among them—
largely in some parts of the country, less so in
others—but even the very slight restriction implied
by the institution is not observed. The intercourse
of the sexes is, in fact, promiscuous; and the law
of inheritance in Bootán has reflectively laid down

that, on the death of a Booteáh, his property is to go to the Deb or Dhurm Rájáh, and not to the children, it being impossible to determine whose children they are. The religion followed is greatly influenced by the peculiar situation and pursuits of the people. In Bootán itself they are all followers of Buddha, or the Llámá; but those inhabiting the Doárs have for a long time accepted many Hindu prejudices and superstitions.

THE MECHES.

The Meches inhabit the forest portion of the Nepál Terái, and are neighbours on the hill side of the Booteáhs, Lepchás, and Limboos, and on the plain side of the Koches and the Dhimáls, of whom the latter are now nearly extinct. They are nomads of Mongolian descent, and resemble the Booteáhs in form, features, and language; and their position on the frontier has always been that of slaves to the Booteáhs. Being quiet and inoffensive, they have accepted this condition with meekness; but they have taken advantage. of their migratory habits gradually to spread further to the south beyond Booteáh influence, and now occupy a large portion of Central and Lower Assam. They hold small estates direct from the Government, and cultivate them principally with cotton, just in the same fashion as the Lepchás, but paying greater attention to their tillage. They are very good-tempered and cheerful, and so inured to labour that no amount of work ever makes them unhappy. At present they are noted for their weakness; but they have tales among them which speak of the achievements of their fathers with the bow and arrows among the wild beasts. For trade they have no aptness, and military service they eschew; but they are not constitutionally apathetic, and are very healthy to look at. The air of the Terái, which is so hurtful to others, suits them best; and they have never attempted to get into higher ranges, the climate of which, they say, does not agree with them. Their habits and manners are modified according to the neighbourhood they live in. In the upper parts of the Terái they eat everything; but they do not eat cows, buffaloes, and fowls within the pale of Hindu influence. Alongside of the Assamese they copy the Assam habits faithfully, and chew *pán* and opium and smoke tobacco to excess, drinking spirits also, though not inordinately. The actual state of society among them is still rather primitive. The men and women share equally in the labours of the field, but beyond weaving, which is practised by the women, they do not know much of the industrial arts. They have commenced to learn these, nevertheless, wherever they have come in contact with the Hindus, and there is little doubt that they will finally be absorbed among them. Their women are decidedly prepossessing, and have a fine complexion and expressive eyes; and daughters are

much prized by their parents because they are a
source of wealth to them, as a wife has always to be
purchased. The female dress is the Bengali *sáree*,
but made generally of red silk. The unmarried
youths of both sexes have sleeping quarters distinct
from their family residences, each at one end of their
village, so that they are kept as widely asunder as
possible. But they nevertheless manage to get
together to make love, and marriage with them
always takes the form of forcible abduction, after
which the bride is retained by her ravisher for some
days. An arrangement is then come to between him
and her parents, by which the latter recognise the union
on the price of their daughter being paid to them.
Polygamy is unknown, and infidelity uncommon;
while prostitution takes the form of *niká* marriages,
by which all widows are disposed of. The religion
professed by the race is the Sivite form of Hinduism;
but their manners and customs are their own and
have nothing in common with it, as is exemplified, for
instance, by the *niká* marriage custom referred to;
which is a Mahomedan and not a Hindu institution.
They have, also, neither castes nor Bráhmans among
them; and, what is more, they sacrifice pigs and fowls
at the shrine of Káli and to their household and river
gods, which the most unorthodox Hindu could never
venture to imitate. They are, in fact, passing through
a transition state now, verging decidedly towards Hinduism, though still remaining at a great distance from it.

L

THE KOCHES.

The Koch race of northern Bengal were very powerful before the Mahomedan conquest of India, and even now are semi-independent, and have a rájáh, or ruler, of their own. Their present nucleus is Cooch Behár, but stragglers from their body are to be met with in several parts of Assam, and in all the country from Rungpore to the hills. The primitive or Páni Koches lived amid the woods, but there are few of them now to be met with. Where still existing they claim to be of the same race with the Gáros, and the language and customs of the two peoples certainly do agree to a great extent. The intermarriage of the other Koch tribes with the Hindus has very considerably civilised them, so much so that their original character can hardly be distinguished at present with certainty. They resemble the Bengalis now more than any other people, except that they breed hogs and poultry and eat them, and make a fermented liquor to drink, which Bengalis of the higher classes do not. The cultivation among the Koches is mainly with the hoe; but they weed their crops, which is not usual with the cognate races around them. Their clothing is made by their women, and is generally coloured blue bordered with red, the material being cotton of their own growth; and they are certainly better clothed than the mass of Hindus around them.

Their huts are also well made, though not raised
on posts like the houses of the Indo-Chinese races
generally. The only arms they carry are spears; but
they are scarcely ever used even against wild beasts.
Their devotion to the sex is peculiar: they leave to
women all the cares of property, and the women in
return are most industrious in weaving, spinning,
brewing, planting, and sowing: in a word, in doing
everything not above their strength. When a woman
dies the property is divided among her daughters;
and when a man marries he goes to live with his
wife's mother, and obeys her as dutifully as his wife
does. Re-marriage of widows is allowed; and widows
left with property can always get young men for
their second and subsequent husbands. The mass
of the race have long become Mahomedans, and
our description here has reference only to the small
remnant of it that still bears the old tribal name.
One clan of the tribe, the Rájbunsis, worship Hindu
deities and have adopted Hindu manners, and the
Rájáh of Cooch Behár belongs to it. He has been
to England, and has married the daughter of a
Bengali gentleman, Mr. Keshub Chunder Sen, the
Bráhmo Apostle, and a thorough reorganisation of
the race may fairly be expected from him.

CHAPTER III.

TRIBES ON THE NORTH-EASTERN FRONTIER.

FROM the east of Bootán to the farthest extremity of Assam the Himálayas are occupied by a great variety of wild tribes, with all of whom the British Government has not yet come into contact. The surface of the country is almost uniformly represented by a confused medley of mountains and narrow valleys, watered by innumerable hill-streams, and the authority of the Government over it is so indefinite that the exterior frontier line has not even been attempted to be laid down. In general the mountains are clothed with magnificent forests infested by savage inhabitants, and all that has been secured to the present time is a very superficial dominion over those of them that live at the base of the outer hills, who receive stipends from the Government in various shapes for such submission or forbearance as they have agreed to. Their title to black-mail was an old privilege enjoyed by them under the native Governments of Assam, which the British Government, on coming to the possession of that country, was obliged to commute into the annual money payments now made, as the raiding propensities of the tribes could not otherwise be controlled. The chief of these peoples are: the Ákhás, Duflás, Meeris, Mishmees, and Ábors, who occupy the upper valley of the Brahmapootra, while, *vis-à-vis* to them, the southern valley is inhabited by the Khámptis, Singphos, and Nágás, who divide the British and Burman dominions from each other. To the west of the Nágás are the Cossyáhs and Gáros, and also the Cácháresc, Meekirs, and Kookies, the latter running south by the Hylákándy valley to the frontier of Chittagong. All these tribes are yet exceedingly wild, and it will take many years of direct interference with them to improve their condition. On the south of the Brahmapootra the policy of permanent occupation and direct management has already been inaugurated in the Nágá, Gáro, Cossyáh and Jynteáh, and Chittagong Hill-tracts, as annexation there does not involve any indefinite extension of responsibility; but the difficulty on the northern side is that the same course cannot be there followed without trenching unduly on the independent States of Thibet and Bootán.

THE ÁKHÁS.

The Ákhás come immediately after the Booteáhs, and have the characteristics of a Mongolian descent prominently developed in a broad round face, flat nose, and small eyes. They are not a very numerous people; but have the credit of being extremely savage, and used at one time to be much feared for their daring raids, especially by their nearest neighbours, the inhabitants of Chárdwár. They are divided into two primary clans—namely, the Házári-Kháwá Ákhás, or "hearth eaters," and the Káppáchore Ákhás or "cotton stealers," both of whom were great outlaws, and defied the power of the zemindárs with impunity. This led to an expedition being undertaken against them in 1836, and to the conclusion of an arrangement by which their good conduct was secured by the payment of pensions to their chiefs: and the oaths then taken have hitherto been generally respected. They are so uncivilised that they do not know how to cultivate; but they tend flocks and herds, and live on them, eating the flesh of cows without touching the milk, which they abominate. Their arms are: the spear, bow and arrows, and a sharp sword, or *dáo*, which is used for all purposes. Of religion their idea is very indistinct; but they fear their mountains and torrents, and the dense jungles in which their cattle go astray. The dead are buried by them, and the spirits of their deceased ancestors are venerated.

THE DUFLÁS.

The Duflás are the nearest neighbours of the Ákhás to the east, and are believed to belong to

the same family, both being again held to be
nearly akin to the Hill Meeris. They are shorter
in stature than both the Ákhás and the Meeris,
and inferior to them in *physique;* but their habits
and manners are in several respects identical with
those of the other tribes. The subdivision into
clans among them is very great, and it is still
believed by many that they are not so much a
single tribe as a collection of numerous cognate
clans almost incapable of combining with each
other. They are nevertheless always much feared
as plunderers, and at one time it was found
necessary to establish a line of military posts
along the frontier to prevent their raids. The
operations of 1836, which were directed against
them as much as against the Ákhás, led to the
same successful results in both cases. Their good
conduct was secured by money payments, and
since then they have very successfully cultivated
the plains they harried. They are rich also in
flocks and herds now, even more than the Ákhás;
but here their superiority over them ceases.
Polygamy exists among both tribes; but polyandry
is far more common among the Duflás, and chastity
almost unknown.

THE MEERIS.

Beyond the Duflás are found, in the lower ranges,
the Meeris, and, in the upper ranges, the Ábors, to

whom the Meeris owed a kind of fealty in former days. The assertion of British authority in Assam relieved the Meeris from this thraldom, and they took advantage of it to remove themselves beyond the pale of Ábor influence to the quarters they now occupy. The Ábors made many applications to the Government authorities to send back to them their runaway slaves, and the lack of any response was one main cause of the unfriendly bearing they subsequently exhibited. The Meeris are believed to be of the same stock with the Ábors, and are tall, powerful men, with the Mongolian features strikingly developed. Their usual head-dress is a cap of cane or bamboo work, covered with tiger or leopard skin, including the tail, which hangs down the back. The nether garment is the *kopti*, which is passed between the legs and fastened to a girdle of canework, while the upper robe is a cloth wrapped round the body and pinned so as to resemble a coat. The women wear a small petticoat made of filaments of cane woven together; and this is often their only garment. The Hill Meeris are rudely armed with *dáos*, and bows and arrows, the last tipped with a deadly vegetable poison; but the Meeris of the plains have always followed peaceful occupations mainly, and go unarmed; and, since they have been relieved of their dependence on the Ábors, have become very prosperous traders and cultivators, the women sharing in field labours with the men. The grounds set apart for cultivation by them are always divided into patches, of which about one-fifth are cultivated at a time, each patch for two years, and every patch in its turn. Fresh ground is never broken so long as the available fallow is found to be sufficient. The crops raised are : *aous* rice, millet, maize, yams, sweet potatoes, tobacco, and red pepper. They also breed pigs and cattle, and rear poultry, and, having no caste prejudices, eat them, though from their intercourse with the Assamese they try to imitate them in most other respects. It is said that they eat even the flesh of tigers; but they do not allow their women to share this food with them, lest it should make them too strong-minded for control! Combining for mutual support, they live in communities, under hereditary chiefs, and occasionally one chief is acknowledged as the highest over a cluster of communities. Their houses are well-made, and have raised floors, with space underneath for their pigs and poultry. One long apartment in each building is used by the whole family to eat, drink, and sleep in, while other portions of it are partitioned off for various domestic purposes; but the fear of the Ábors is still so great that the family valuables are invariably kept buried. Their granaries, on the contrary, are always kept unprotected in the midst of their fields, the villagers having perfect confidence in each other's good faith and honesty. Polygamy

is practised among them, especially by the chiefs ;
and, after the death of a chief, his son becomes
the husband of all his widows, except of the mother
who bore him. Instances of polyandry are also
known. All the girls, in fact, have their prices,
the largest price for the best-looking girl varying
from twenty to thirty pigs, and, if one man cannot
give so many, he has no objection to take partners
to make up the number.

THE ABORS.

The Ábors lie to the north of the Meeris up to
the borders of Thibet, and are a blunt, independent,
and warlike people, much feared by all their neighbours. They call themselves *Pádam*, the name
Ábor—" rude or barbarous "—having been given to
them by the Assamese. Apparently they are of the
same race with the Meeris and the Duflás, or, at all
events, there is no very material difference between
them. The distinct sects and settlements of the
Ábors are many, the most important of them being
the Bor, Membu, Silook, Sissee, Pádoo, Páshee, and
Bomjeer tribes respectively. In general terms, they
are regarded as confederate states ; but each community is governed by its own laws, devised and
administered on purely democratic principles. The
laws are made by the people collected together,
every individual having an equal vote. No chief
is expressly acknowledged ; but there are always a

few persons in every community who, either from superior wealth, hereditary distinction, or real ability, exert strong influence over the rest, swaying them almost as they list. Membu is the largest of the settlements known, but those occupying the loftier ranges behind are believed to be of greater consequence, especially the Bor Ábors, who seem to be the most powerful. The contact of the British Government with the Ábors is of comparatively recent date. The first expedition against them was sent up in 1859, and another was got ready in 1861, when overtures were received for a peaceful arrangement of differences. Several communities came in, and, in consideration of the democratic nature of their unions, payment in kind to the communities was agreed to instead of money payments to the chiefs, a change which gave to each individual an interest in keeping the peace.

The appearance of the Ábors is not very prepossessing. They are nearly as tall as the Meeris, but are clumsy-looking and sluggish. Their features are Mongolian; and they have deep sepulchral voices. The women resemble the Chinese to some extent in features and complexion, but are of a coarser type, and many of them are disfigured with *goître*. The dress of the men consists of a *dhoti* made of the bark of the *udddl* tree, which also serves the purposes of a carpet to sit upon and of a covering. It is tied round the loins, and hangs down behind in loose

strips like a white bushy beard, and is used too as
a pillow at night by being rolled up.   The rest of
his equipment depends entirely on the taste of each
individual.   Some wear plain basket caps; others
have cane caps covered with skins; others, again,
use caps of helmet fashion.   Almost every man has a
woollen coat, while those who have not are dressed
in skins; and necklaces of blue beads are worn as
ornaments.   The female dress is a piece of cloth
suspended by a string round the loins, and reaching
to the knees, while another piece is folded round
the bosom, though this latter is often dispensed
with in hot weather, the exposure of the person
above the waist not being considered indelicate.
The decorations worn by both men and women are
strings of beads, which, in the case of the latter,
reach from the neck to the waist; and enormous
earrings of nearly an inch in diameter, to make
place for which the lobes of the ear are gradually
distended and enlarged from childhood.   The women
add to these anklets of cane tightly laced, so as to
set off the fine swell of their legs, the canes being
sometimes tinged with a light-blue colour to heighten
the effect; and a row of embossed plates of bell
metal is worn as an undergarment, suspended from
the loins—but by young females only, till they
become mothers.   The hair of both sexes is cropped
close, by lifting it up on a knife and chopping it
all round with a stick; and both 'men and women

are tattooed, many bearing the mark of the cross on the forehead, though not as an emblem of salvation, notwithstanding the assumption of some observers that the earlier fathers of the Church who operated in India might perhaps have converted their ancestors ! The arms of the warriors are spears, long straight swords, daggers, and crossbows and arrows, the last used with or without poison ; and their caps and helmets are ornamented with the hair of the yak dyed red, boar's tusks, and the beak of the buceros. The salute of an Ábor chief is usually a shrill whoop, not unlike the crowing of a cock ; and in their meetings in council this cry is every now and then renewed, while the right foot is made to break the ground constantly—like that of a pawing steed.

In disposition the Ábors are said to be like tigers—so much so, that they cannot live alongside of each other in peace. Their houses are accordingly scattered, singly or in groups of two or three at most, all over the mountainous country they inhabit. The huts are, as a rule, well made and convenient, though not very roomy. Their cultivation is almost all in the plains, and consists of rice, cotton, tobacco, maize, ginger, red pepper, a great variety of esculent roots and pumpkins, and the sugar cane. To these they have added opium, the use of which is increasing. They do not break new lands unnecessarily. When the land they were cultivating gets exhausted,

they revert to that which was lying fallow, whereby
the whole space from their village to the most distant
point of their cultivation gets cleared and appropriated while the rest of the forest is spared. The
boundaries of each man's clearing are denoted by
upright stones, and property in cultivated or fallow
land is recognised and respected. Their implements
of husbandry are long knives and swords, crooked
bamboos to scrape the earth with, and pointed sticks
to make holes, into which they dexterously shoot the
seed grains to be sown. In all agricultural labours
the men are assisted by their wives; but the entire
work does not devolve on the women, as among
some other tribes. They also know the art of
working iron, and make their own *dáos* and bells,
some of which they export. The most common
occupation of all, however, is hunting; and they eat
the flesh of every animal they kill, including that of
the elephant, the rhinoceros, and the buffalo, but
express an abhorrence of beef. They drink a fermented liquor prepared by themselves, but have a
marked partiality for brandy if they can get it,
and are rather intemperate drinkers. The women
among them are well treated, though hardworked;
and polygamy, if permitted, is not usually practised.
This, however, seems peculiar to the Pádoo community especially. Among the Sissee Ábors a man
has often as many wives as he can afford to buy.
Polyandry is also practised; and a common rule

with the Sissees is for two or three brothers to have a number of wives in common. Marriages are ostensibly arranged by parents ; but, in point of fact, the young people concerned always settle the affair between themselves—seldom marrying, however, out of their own clan. A feast is the only ceremony observed, besides which the lover has to find such exquisite delicacies as field mice and squirrels for his mistress and her parents. In demeanour the women are equally free from timidity and levity ; but they are at the same time totally devoid of modesty, and chastity is not an Ábor virtue. Of their religion all that is certainly known is that they sacrifice to a great number of deities supposed to reside in their woods and mountains, and believe in a future state of rewards and punishments. They have no medicine for the sick: for every disease there is a spirit who has to be mollified. The sacrifices are necessarily constant ; and every sacrifice furnishes an excuse for a debauch.

THE MISHMEES.

The hills which close the north-east corner of Assam are occupied by the Mishmees, a short sturdy race, of fair complexion and great activity, whose features betray a cross between the Mongolian and the Hindu. Though extremely wild-looking, they are comparatively inoffensive; but they are exceedingly dirty, and almost equally dishonest.

.They are divided into a vast number of petty clans, of whom the Choolkáttá, the Táen, and the Myjoo are the most important. The Choolkáttás, or "crop-haired," are the most western, and occupy the mountains on the banks of the Dibong; and they are also reputed to be the most savage. The Táens extend eastward from the Choolkáttás, and the Myjoos eastward after them, being the most remote. The warlike clans are the Choolkáttás and the Myjoos, while the Táens and several smaller tribes, called the Mároos, Manneáhs, Tshees, Dháhs, Mlees, etc., have always been decidedly peaceful. They are altogether a numerous people, but exceedingly indigent, and ill-provided both with food and clothing. Agriculture is carried on by them in the most rude and simple manner, and their supply of food-grains is necessarily scanty. They are richer in flocks and herds, and are so dependent on animal food for subsistence that no animal, from an elephant to a mouse, comes amiss to them. The dress of all classes is very inferior, and that of the lower orders scarcely decent; but the chiefs wrap themselves in comfortable long cloaks of Thibet wool, besides wearing an apology for a *dhoti* round the loins. The female dress is more copious, consisting of a coloured *sáree* wrapped round the waist and a rather scanty bodice sometimes covered with a thicker garment. Both men and women wear the hair long, and have it turned up into a knot on the crown of the head; but the

Choolkáttás crop the hair in front, which makes them hideous to look at. The head-dress of all tribes is either a fur cap or a wicker helmet; and the weapons usually carried are a spear or a cross-bow, and a large heavy knife, which helps them to open out passages through their jungles. By far the most remarkable article of their equipment, however, is the earring, which is quite as massive as that worn by the Ábors. They also carry a pouch of monkey's skin at the girdle, to carry tobacco and a case of flint and stone, and have always a pipe in their mouth, even women and children barely five years old being partial to the weed. The ornaments of the women consist of a profusion of beads worn as a necklace, mixed with colourless glass and oblong pieces of coarse cornelian; a thin plate of silver fixed on the head; and earrings as thick as or even thicker than those worn by the men, with a triangular plate of silver suspended from each, which remains in the direction of the shoulders.

The habitations of the Mishmees are hid in jungles, and are built apart from each other, as they do not congregate in villages. They are usually erected on slopes, resting on one side on the hill-face and on the other on poles driven into the ground. Those belonging to the chiefs are very long and about twelve feet in breadth. One side of each hut is partitioned off to exhibit the skulls of the animals on which the owner had in the course of his life feasted his friends, while the other is divided into smaller apartments, in all of which one or more hearths are always blazing. The house and its inmates are, for this reason, always black with dust and smoke, the more so as the latter are not over-fond of ablutions. At one time this people caused much trouble by their depredations, but they are now best known on the frontier as keen traders only, every man among them having converted himself into a petty merchant. Their country is, for the most part, very rugged and difficult to travel in; but they are never tired of moving about in their trading expeditions, and for many years no greater crime has been traced to them than kidnapping women and children, where they can get at them, to sell them into slavery. Some of them are clever manufacturers, and utilise the fibrous plants growing wild in their hills for the preparation of stiff cloths. One species of cloth made by them is so strong that it serves as a sort of armour in war; and every cloth they weave sells well, the Ábors being their principal customers. They are known as being sharp in their dealings generally, and most of them are deceitful also; and the practice of using poisoned arrows in fight has always been common with them. Exchange of dress, however, gives birth to, or is a sign of, amity; and by exchange of weapons the most deadly enemies become fast friends, and if one falls in fight it becomes the duty of the other to avenge his death

and recover his skull. Polygamy prevails largely
among all the tribes, the number of a man's wives
being held* to be the test of his wealth and
consequence. The women are very comely, but
mostly of indifferent character. Wives are, in fact,
not expected to be chaste, and are not thought worse
of when they are otherwise; and, as among the
Meeris, the son of a Mishmee always succeeds to
the use of his father's widows, his own mother only
going over to the next of kin among the males. The
religion of the race is confined to the propitiation
of demons and sylvan deities, the most feared of all
being the god of destruction; and pigs and fowls are
sacrificed to them.

THE KHÁMPTIS.

Crossing the Brahmapootra we come to the
Khámptis and the Singphos, both colonies of the
Shán race of Burmáh, who came to Assam from
the sources of the Irráwádi. They are found in
and about Sudiyá, the extreme north-eastern corner
of Assam, where the Khámptis are said to have
settled in A.D. 1750. The Bor Khámptis of the Irráwádi, from whom they claim immediate descent,
are a numerous and powerful people by whom
the Burmese army is largely recruited, and the
Assam branch of the tribe are also tall and well
made. They were, however, not a very graceful
race at the outset, and even now, though their

M 2

intermarriage with the Assamese has somewhat
softened and improved their features, their women are
very plain-looking, if not ugly. They make themselves uglier by turning up their hair into a knot
on the centre of the head, a fashion common to
both sexes; but the natural profusion of their
tresses necessarily makes the knots of the women
bigger and therefore more hideous. The dress
of both men and women is decent, the nether
garments being a *dhoti* of chequered pattern, or
silk, which the women wear as a petticoat. The
upper clothing of the men is a tight-fitting jacket
usually dyed blue, and a white turban ; while
the women wear a looser jacket and a coloured
scarf over it. The ornaments in use are all made
of metal and small glass beads. The arms of the
men are the *dáo* for all offensive purposes, and a
shield, some carrying China-made matchlocks also
where they have got them. But they are not much
given to martial pursuits at present. They are the
most civilised of all the mountain tribes in Assam, and are everywhere very peacefully employed
in field-work, house-building, working in metals,
marketing, and the like ; and are said to understand a little of reading and writing also. They
rear pigs and fowls in abundance, and hold weekly
markets to dispose of their surplus stocks, the
articles usually consisting of pigs, fowls, eggs, dried
fish, salt, ginger, onions, tobacco, and *dáos*.   The

currency of the country is the *dáo*, and also unwrought iron. The marketing is conducted in an
orderly and business-like manner, without any
of the haggling and driving a bargain so common
in Hindu *bazárs*. The buyers and sellers are
separated into groups for the sale of each article, so
that the buyer has every variety of the article he
requires exposed before him. In their field labours
the men are much assisted by their wives, and the
out-turn is ordinarily abundant. Their houses are
always well and strongly built of sound timber, with
raised floors and thatched roofs, and some of the
buildings, especially their temples, are delicately
carved. This finds work even for their chiefs, who
also have apt hands for embroidery, and amuse themselves moreover by manufacturing silver pipes, brass
bowls, and other nick-nacks of the same kind, which
are said to be neatly made. The religion professed
by the race is Buddhism, as it is understood in
Burmáh; and their chief festivals have reference to
the birth and death of Gautama. Polygamy is
permitted, but seldom availed of; and the women
have every liberty allowed to them, and are well-
treated.

THE SINGPHOS.

The Singphos are a more powerful race than the
Khámptis, nominally divided into twelve *gáums*, or
clans, of whom three or four are considered to be the

most influential, though they are all quite independent of each other, and never unite except in the prosecution of a common purpose. Each clan is, in fact, wholly governed by its chief, and acts separately for, with, or against the others as circumstances or inclination may direct. Much trouble was caused by all of them on the frontier at one time, and even now their life is not altogether peaceful, though they are catching civilisation quickly from the Khámptis. The men are somewhat better looking than the Khámptis, though having features of the same type, and are very athletic and capable of enduring great fatigue; but their women, who work with them, though actually of more pleasing features than the Khámpti women, very soon become coarse-looking from the hard labour devolving on them. The dress of both sexes is nearly the same with that of the Khámptis, and they wear their hair also after the same manner, in a knot on the crown of the head, except that the unmarried girls gather it in a roll resting on the back of the neck. Both men and women tattoo their limbs, the women more largely than the men, which disfigures them to a greater degree. The arms of the men, like those of the Khámptis, consist of the *dáo*, the shield, and the matchlock, and include in addition the crossbow and arrows; and their occupations, too, are very similar, the Singphos being only more partial to iron-smelting than to any other work. The *dáos* they make are very highly prized all over the frontier, and get rapid sale; and they also make their own apparel. The country they occupy is low and extremely fertile, and rice, sugar-cane, and corn thrive well upon it; but, cultivation having long been neglected in it, owing to the original predatory habits of the people, it is at present largely overgrown with jungle. The religion of the people is Buddhism, of the same shape as of the Khámptis; and they believe also in malignant spirits, who are propitiated with sacrifices. Polygamy is extensively practised, and, besides the wives married, slaves are retained, the offspring of both having equal rights. The law of succession is peculiar, too, in another way—it gives to the eldest son all the landed property of the father, to the youngest all his personal property, while the rest inherit nothing; and this division is made without reference to the mother's status or nationality. The dead are buried, and the bodies of the chiefs are kept in state often for two or more years, in a coffin which is surrounded with the insignia of the rank held by them in life; and the process of decomposition leaves nothing beyond the bones to inter.

THE NÁGÁS.

The Nágás lie to the south-west of the Khámptis and the Singphos, being scattered all over the mountain ridge that divides Assam from Munipore.

The word "Nágá" means a serpent, but it is not pretended that the Nágás are of serpent or Scythic descent. The name was more probably given to them originally as being best expressive of their character, for of all wild tribes they are held to be the most subtle and treacherous. There are about a dozen septs of them, who differ considerably from each other in several respects, each having some distinct peculiarity of its own and often a distinct language. Those of the upper ranges are generally light-coloured and handsome, and their women pretty, though beauty of form is not the rule of the hills; but those of the lower ranges, such as the Lotáh Nágás and others, are dark, dirty, and squat. The differences in character also are equally prominent, for, while the Rengmá Nágás are spoken of as being good-natured, peaceful, and honest, the Lotáhs are known as unsocial and sulky, and the Ángámis as contentious, vindictive, and perfidious. The Nágás *par excellence* are the last, whose name *Angámi*, or the "unconquered," is their boast. They live high up the mountains, and have always distinguished themselves as caterans and murderers, and also for being perpetually at feud with each other, their feuds going down from generation to generation. Their villages are accordingly planned for everyday defence and stockaded as hill-forts, from which barbarous onslaughts are made, in which neither age nor sex is spared. They gave a world of trouble to the

Government by the many plundering inroads they
made on the peaceful tribes occupying the foot of
their hills; and several expeditions had to be sent
against them, commencing from 1835. In 1865, the
location of a special officer in their hills was
determined upon, and the country taken under
direct management, after which its history was
rather uneventful for a long time, though never
altogether peaceful. Subsequently some outrages
were perpetrated in 1879, in connexion with an
attempt to dislodge the British authority from the
hills, and culminated In the murder of the special
officer, Mr. Damant, and his escort, which led to
an expedition being undertaken against the savages
by General Nation, and to their punishment. Peace
has since been ostensibly restored; but it is hardly
to be supposed that it will be long preserved. The
bellicose disposition of the race has not yet been
mastered, and what seems calculated to master
it in the future even more than Government interference is tea-planting, the operations connected
with which are gradually spreading British rule over
the immense wastes now held by these people, the
limits of which are likely to be extended in the end
to Munipore on the south, and on the east to the
Pátkoi range and the borders of Burmáh and China.
The Nágás are carrying on a most profitable business
with the tea gardens, and those so engaged have
already been partially humanised, at the same time

1

70   THE WILD TRIBES OF INDIA.

that their occupation has forced them to neglect their internal bickerings.

The Nágás are a fine, stalwart race, though inferior in *physique* as compared with the tribes inhabiting the north of the Brahmapootra, having smaller bones and much less of muscular development. Their faces are lozenge-shaped, features flat, eyes small, complexion dark; and of hair they have none in the shape of beard, whisker, or moustache, while that on the head is cut short and trained to stand erect. But, despite these drawbacks, their carriage is dignified, and they have over all a wild expression peculiar to them, which distinguishes them from all other tribes in their vicinity. The females are short and waistless, but not necessarily ungainly, though they are too hard-worked to retain any shade of comeliness long, having every employment, apart from fighting, hunting, and traffic, saddled on them. There is no clothing for either sex in the higher elevations, and hence some imagine that the name Nágá may, perhaps, have been derived from the word "Lungá," or naked. At the foot of the hills the limbs are usually covered with a small piece of cloth dyed with indigo, a larger piece of coarse cloth being also used for covering the body when needed; while nearer the tea gardens the men wear kilts of different patterns and colours, and the women picturesque petticoats, and a cotton *chádur* thrown across the back and chest. They are very fond of

ornaments at all places, and both males and females
go loaded with them, the trinkets consisting of necklaces, bracelets, and armlets, made mainly of cowries,
and more rarely of greenish beads which are particularly prized. What the Nágá most of all delights
in, however, are his weapons, which are his constant
companions, awake and sleeping. These are: the
ddo, or battle-axe, the spear or javelin, and the shield
—for he never uses the bow and arrows. The Ángámis
have also long known the use of firearms, of which
they have got a considerable supply. Fighting and
hunting, however, are not their sole occupations at
the present day. They understand the advantages
of trading, and frequently come down to the markets
of Assam and Cáchár heavily laden with ivory, wax,
and cloths manufactured from the nettle-fibre, in
exchange for which they receive salt, brassware, and
shells, and, by preference, matchlocks and gunpowder
if they can get them. Their only other occupations
are dancing and debauch, both of which are sometimes, not always, shared in by their women. The
war-dance in particular is performed by the men
alone, with spear and hatchet in hand, while all the
circumstances of battle are acted, namely, the advance, retreat, wielding of weapons, and defence
with the shield, accompanied by terrific howls and
war-whoops.

As the Nágás are not a migratory people, like
the other hillmen around them, their villages are

stationary and unchanging, and those marked in Rennel's Maps of 1764 are still to be found. Some of them are very large, containing so many as five hundred houses, and there are none which have less than fifty. The houses are built after a peculiar fashion, having the eaves down to the ground, while one gable-end forms the door to enter by. Every family has a separate house, and each house generally contains two rooms, one for sleeping in, and the other for all other purposes, including the custody of pigs and fowls. The accommodation is necessarily straitened, and the unmarried young men of the family have to sleep out of it, all the bachelors of a village being accommodated in one common building, furnished with a series of bamboo beds covered with mats. In this house are also exhibited the spoils of the chase and the implements of war belonging to the community; and it is further used as the village inn, in which travellers from other villages are allowed to put up. The separation of the sexes in youth, if intended, is not, however, actually very rigidly enforced, young men and women having every facility given to them to become well acquainted with each other; and when they have made up their minds to marry they are at once united, the only form gone through being the execution of a contract of union by both parties, unattended by any religious ceremony whatever. Presents are then made by the bridegroom to the family of the bride, and there is a grand feast given to the whole village, in return for which the villagers have to build a house for the accommodation of the youthful pair. Divorces and remarriages are both allowed and freely availed of, and open infidelity is necessarily not of frequent occurrence.

As a rule the Nágá woman is a model of labour and industry, and is mainly valued on that account. She does everything the husband will not, and he considers it effeminate to do anything but fight, hunt, and cheat. The cultivation labours are all performed by the wife, the crops raised consisting of rice, cotton, and tobacco, as well as several kinds of vegetables. She also weaves, both with cotton and with nettle-fibres, and manufactures salt from the many salt-springs in the country, though she is not able to make it at less cost than is charged for the salt sent up from Bengal. The tending of cows, goats, pigs, and fowl likewise devolves on her in most places, and she of course cooks and performs every other household work besides. One curious way of cooking with some clans is thus described in Owen's *Nágá Tribes:*—" Their manner of cooking is performed in joints of bamboos, introduced into which are as much rice, chillies, and meat, with water, as each will hold and can be thrust tightly in by the aid of a stick. A couple of bamboos placed on the ground, with a third connecting them at the top horizontally, constitutes a fire-place, against which those holding the food rest.

By continually turning the bamboos the food becomes well roasted, and is then served out on leaves from a neighbouring tree." Neither milk nor any preparation thereof is appreciated by the Nágás generally, but they eat animals of all kinds, including rats, snakes, monkeys, tigers, and elephants; and the roast dog in particular is regarded as a great delicacy. Another article equally prized is a liquor manufactured from fermented rice, which is drunk by both sexes in great quantities; they are inveterate smokers also, and are especially fond of the oil of tobacco, which they mix with water and drink.

The Nágás have no kind of internal government, and acknowledge no supreme authority. If spoken to on the subject they plant their javelin on the ground and declare that to be their Rájáh, and that they will have none other. The *Gdou Boord*, or elder of the village, has some authority conceded to him; but it is very moderate, and is often resisted and defied. A council of elders is suffered to adjust petty disputes and disagreements, but only in the way of arbitration. There is no constituted authority lodged anywhere in the community; every man doing what he likes and is able to perform. The Nágá is by nature fierce as the tiger, and matters are necessarily made worse from the total want of control over his passions. His other vices are drunkenness and thieving, in the latter of which he glories, though it is held very dishonourable to be discovered in the act. His religion consists in the worship of a plurality of deities, or good and evil spirits, to whom sacrifices are made, and in the belief in omens, by which his conduct is mainly guided. The chief religious festival is called the Genná, a Sabbath extended generally over two or three days and nights, when all the inhabitants of the village celebrating it live in complete isolation from others, sacrificing and drinking, but not permitting any one to witness their debaucheries. There is no fixed time for this ceremony, which is frequently repeated in the course of the year—that is, whenever it is considered necessary to make propitiatory offerings to their gods. The dead among them are buried at the doors of their own houses, and the spear and *dáo* of the warrior are always buried with him.

THE CÁCHÁRESE.

The district which has suffered most from the Nágá raids is Cáchár, which, within a small confined area, holds several tribes pushed into it from different directions. Of these the most important are : the Cáchárese, the minor Nágá tribes, the Meekirs, and the Kookies.

The Cáchárese are a large race whose proper name is Rangtsá, and their original country that situated to the north-east of Assam. They were at one time limited to Cáchár, and still form the dominant class

of the district, but are now also scattered all over
Assam; and even the Hájongs of Mymensing are
held to be a branch of the same family. They are
a fine hardy race, quiet, industrious, and thriving, and
have strongly marked Mongolian features. Both men
and women wear the hair long, but even full-grown
men have no beard or whiskers. The primary
divisions of the race are two—namely, the Hazái, or
people of the plains, and the Purbutteáhs, or people
of the hills. The former profess to be Hindus, but
eat pigs and fowls, and even sacrifice them to their
gods, with the exception of the Seroniáh, or "the
purified," who have adopted Hindu prejudices in
regard to food in their integrity, and the Shargiah,
or "the heavenly," who border on Thibet and
Bootán, and have accepted Llámáism with all its
conventionalities. The chief occupation of the race
is cultivation; but, while the dwellers of the plains
cultivate with the plough, those of the hills do so
with the hoe only. The jungles among which the
Purbutteáhs live are mainly of bamboos, and these,
being cut down and set on fire, leave a coating of
ashes on the ground, which is the only manure used
to fertilise it. The soil below the ashes is then
turned up with the hoe, and the seeds to be sown are
dropped in—paddy, sugar-cane, cotton, and tobacco
being all sown together in the same ground. Each
plot of ground is cultivated only for two years, after
which it is left untouched for from seven to ten years,

on the expiration of which it is considered to be once more fit for cultivation.

The villages of the Cáchárese comprise from twenty to a hundred houses, each family having a separate dwelling for itself. The bachelors live apart from their families, in a large house in the centre of every village, which is called the *Dekhá chang*, or the warriors' house ; but opportunities are given to them to consort with the maidens, and marriage still preserves the primitive form of abduction. When the lovers have agreed to unite their fortunes together, the bridegroom proceeds with his friends to the house of the bride to get forcible possession of her person. Her friends, affecting surprise, run out to the rescue in haste, and there is a stubborn mock-fight between the parties with no violence committed on either side. Eventually the bridegroom's party proves successful, upon which he gives a feast to the discomfited friends of the bride, and conciliates her father, who is supposed to be mightily incensed, by a money present, which completes the ceremony. The religion of the race, we have already said, is an affectation of Hinduism *minus* its food restrictions. Except the very orthodox, all classes eat meat of all kinds, beef only excepted; they also drink spirits, though in no immoderate degree, and are not unacquainted with the use of opium. The general intelligence of the race is not much to speak of, though the Hazáis

N

affect to have got educated by their connexion with
the Assamese. Diseases are believed to arise from
preternatural agency, and in place of doctors they
have *rojdhs*, or exorcists, to cure them. Witchcraft
is also believed in, and the *rojdh* assists here too in
removing the spell.

THE MEEKIRS.

The Meekirs came originally from the jungles
marked in the maps as Toolarám Senáputty's country, and, like the Cáchárese, are divided into classes,
namely, the hill and plain Meekirs respectively.
They are physically much inferior to the Cáchárese,
and even the hill Meekirs are not warriors. But,
if cowardly, they have the credit of being very
laborious, and raise rice and cotton in abundance,
the latter of which they sell to advantage. The only
weapon they carry is the *ddo*, of which no use is
made except for cultivation and wood cutting. Their
dress consists of two pieces of cotton cloth dyed with
red stripes and sewn together like a bag, with aper-
tures left for the head and arms; and this is put on
in the manner of a shirt. They build their houses
on high *máchdns*, or platforms, and the buildings are
always large, being made to hold some thirty or forty
persons, often of different families, who sleep together
almost in a state of nudity. The chief food of the
tribe consists of rice, pigs, and goats; but they refrain
from eating cows, more from prudential than religious

motives. They also delight in spirituous liquors, which are often drunk to excess; but they are peaceful in their cups, and disturbances seldom occur. Of religion their idea is indefinite, though they affect to have become converted to Hinduism. The objects worshipped are the Sun and Moon, and large rocks and forest trees, which are considered to be the abodes of invisible deities. Animal sacrifices are made at these places and offered up along with boiled rice. For marriage they have no religious ceremony. A bargain is made between the parties proposing to be united, and a contract entered into which makes them man and wife, a feast being given in commemoration of the event. Polygamy is discountenanced, but not expressly forbidden; and widows are allowed to remarry.

THE KOOKIES.

The Kookies are a numerous race whose proper limits have not been defined even to this day. Their original settlements seem to have been in the hill recesses to the south of the Hylákandy valley, a wild and difficult country of large extent, whence they have branched out northwards into Hill Tipperáh, and southwards into Chittagong. The tribes occupying such a large territory are of course various, and are known under different names in different places, such as Lunctás, Chuckmás, Tipperáhs, Reángs, Lusháis, etc, all living independent of each other,

and each ruled over by its own separate chief. The
appellation "Kookie" is equally unknown to all of
them, having been given to them by thē inhabitants
of Eastern Bengal : for their whole race they have no
common name, and are content to call one another
by the names of their different clans. But their
general characteristics are very similar in all places,
and they are easily distinguishable by them from other
tribes. They are all of stout and muscular make,
though of a short size, and have a dark complexion,
flat nose, and small eyes. Of some the legs are
disproportionately short and the arms disproportionately long ; and the face, which in every case is as
broad as it is long, is among some tribes round, but
among others nearly square. The women of all
tribes are equally ungainly and filthy, and more squat
even than the men ; but they are at the same time
very strong and lusty. The dress of the different
tribes varies to some extent according to taste and
locality ; but there is not much room for variation
where the general fashion is to go naked.   According
to their own traditions the Kookies and the Mughs,
or Joomeáhs, are of the same parentage, born of the
same father by different mothers. The mother of the
Kookies dying first, during the infancy of her son, the
child was brought up by his stepmother, who gave
him no clothing, and so he came to be called *Lunctá*,
or "the naked." Where any dress is worn, the women
have a small blue cloth round the loins, reaching

from below the navel to the knee, and another cloth thrown over the shoulders, while the men have their *dhotis* and *meredis*, and a cloth tied round the head which stands for a turban. The women wear no head-dress at any place, but cultivate a luxuriant crop of hair instead of it. The ornaments worn are necklaces, armlets and bracelets made of brass which are very massy, and earrings. The arms of the warriors are the *dáo*, the bow and arrows, and the spear, a shield being occasionally used in addition for defence. Strings are also worn by them around the neck, both as ornament and armour; and tufts of goat-hair dyed red are worn on the thighs. The distinctive mark of the Tipperáhs is a large quill stuck on the back of the head, from which red-coloured goat-hair is hung out in streamers.

The Kookies in Cáchár are divided into two primary septs called the "old" and the "new." The "old" are subdivided into three clans, of whom the most considerable in numbers are the Rhangkol, who are very powerful men physically, and very steady labourers, both for working and carrying. They dress decently, and are fond of ornaments; but, like the rest of their race, neither wash their bodies nor their clothes, and are eaten up with skin diseases. They have no chiefs, but every village has a headman with limited powers. Their notions of religion are mainly borrowed from the Assamese, and are vague;

but marriage is a religious ceremony with them, and always requires the presence of the *Ghálim*, or priest. There is no polygamy among them, and widows have the same liberty as widowers to remarry.

The "new" Kookies were driven into Cáchár by the Lunctás within the recollection of the present generation, some thirty years ago. They are divided into four clans, each having a rájáh, or chief, of its own, who is entitled to receive one out of each brood of pigs or fowls, one quarter of every animal killed in the chase, one tusk of every elephant slain, and one basket of rice from each of his subjects. He is also entitled to receive free labour from each man for four days in the year, and has the privilege of adjusting their quarrels and differences with the assistance of a council of elders and of laws peculiar to the tribe, his decision being final in every case. The religion of the tribe recognises an all-powerful deity named Puthen, who has a wife, a son, and a daughter-in-law; and, in addition to them, there are household gods, to whom sacrifices are made.

The Tipperáhs are Kookies who own allegiance to the Rájáh of Tipperáh, paying him an annual *nussur*, and *abwábs* on marriage and other occasions. They are fairer than the other tribes, some of them being hardly darker than a swarthy European, but are not distinguishable from the rest in any other respect. They pretend to be Hindus, but have no restrictions of caste, and eat almost any kind of food, and from the hands of any person. Pigs, fowls, and pigeons are reared by them; but they keep no oxen, which they do not eat nor know any other use of.

The most powerful of the Kookie tribes are the Lushais, who are also the most easterly; and it is on account of their wars and raids mainly that the other septs have been forced forward into British territory in the directions indicated. The quarrels of the Lushais, like those of the Nágás, are incessant, and, as they always prefer to surprise their enemies instead of attacking them openly, however strong their own party might be, there is no option left to those who are attacked but to fly before them, since their main object is not so much to plunder as to kill or take slaves. Proceeding on a foray, they will march in the night with the stealthy pace of the jackal, in the most profound silence, and on being overtaken by day will so conceal themselves among trees as to remain unperceived by persons passing under them, waiting in ambush till the time for surprise arrives. The only notice given of an attack is the shout by which it is commenced, and those who cannot fly are either killed or carried off. After victory the assailants retire, taking away the heads of the slain and their slaves, the former to be used in certain ceremonies performed at the funerals of their chiefs, and for being exhibited as trophies. But, if they are defeated, they go back to their homes as silently as they came, and live in disgrace till their failure is retrieved. The one well understood law with all of them is that blood can only be wiped out with blood; and, if the murderer be a tiger, the Lushái will rush after him to kill him, and will never be satisfied till he has been killed, cooked, and eaten. Nay, if a man is killed by the fall of a tree, his friends will cut up the tree into chips, or burn it till it is reduced to ashes. The trouble caused on the frontier by a race so vindictive was necessarily great, and, in 1871-72, the Government had to send a rather strong party against them to repress their inroads, which was successful to this extent, that some of the raiding chiefs were punished and accepted the terms that were dictated to them.

The general character of the race is that they are nomadic but gregarious; frequently shifting their grounds, but not so migratory as the Mughs. The latter never remain on the same spot for more than two years; but the Kookie settlements are seldom changed before the expiration of four or five years. Their villages, called *khoadhs*, are therefore always better formed and finished than those of their neighbours. They are usually posted on the steepest and most inaccessible hills, and are fortified with bamboo palisades, while the passages to them are guarded day and night, in peace and war. Precautions of this sort are necessary on account of the aggressive character of the race and the outrages

they perpetrate, which invite reprisals. The houses
in the villages are usually well made, and are raised
on platforms of bamboos some six feet from the
ground, and ranged in rows on each side of a
street. Their cultivation patches also are very
carefully arranged, but the work on these devolves
mostly on their women. The men are all hunters
and warriors, while the women work on the fields,
an occupation from which no rank exempts them,
the wife of a chief working alongside of the wife
of his vassal. The process of cultivation is *jooming*,
and the crops raised are rice and other grains of
various sorts, roots, vegetables, tobacco, and cotton.
The grains and vegetables form the chief food of
the people, besides which they are fond of eating
flesh of all kinds, and rear pigs and poultry. They
also make their own fermented liquors and spirits,
but do not drink intemperately, and are seldom
seen intoxicated. They are more fond of tobacco,
which is smoked not only by men and women, but
also by children ; and, in common with the Nágás,
they drink the oil of tobacco mixed with water.
Of the cotton raised by them the best portion is
sold to the Bengali *bepáris* by barter for fowls,
each fowl being considered equivalent to its weight
of cotton. A prodigious quantity of honey is also
found in their forests, but they do not know how
to separate it from the wax of the comb. In some
places they are so rude that they still kindle fire

by rubbing two pieces of wood together, and use
the ashes of the bamboo as a substitute for salt.
Their greatest of all virtues is valour, and the
only accomplishments worth acquiring are : first,
a knowledge of the military tactics practised by
themselves, and, after it, thieving—the most contemptible of men, however, being, as with the Nágás,
a detected thief. An oath taken by a Kookie is
always held sacred ; but it is very seldom that he
will take any, and never except on very serious
occasions.

The women of the Kookies, as among the Nágás,
are only valued for the amount of labour they
perform. The manner of obtaining a wife is either
by paying a price for her, or, in the old Jewish
fashion, by serving for her in bondage for a term of
years ; but no great value is placed on her rectitude.
Cases of adultery and seduction are inquired into
and punished, the punishment resting with the
husband or father from whose charge the girl may
have been seduced ; but, on the other hand, all the
women of a village, married or unmarried, are available to the chief at his will, and no stigma attaches
to those who are favoured by him. Polygamy is
not permitted ; but there is no objection to retaining
concubines in addition to a wife. The marriage
arrangements on behalf of the female are usually
made by her father, and his inquiries in regard to
her lover are best answered when the answer is

that he is a great warrior, a good hunter, and an expert thief. The proofs demanded, and which have to be shown, are the heads of the enemies slain by him, the heads of the game he may have killed, and the goods in his house that were stolen. If these are forthcoming, the arrangements are at once concluded. The idea of religion among all tribes is very similar to that entertained by the "new" Kookies of Cáchár, except that the wilder Kookies believe more largely in spirits having charge of their forests, hills, and rivers, than in household deities, and that the best sacrifice a man can make to them is the heads of his enemies. Their idea of Paradise represents a happy hunting-ground, where rice grows spontaneously, and game abounds as the heritage of the man who has killed the largest number of his enemies in life, the people killed by him attending on him as his slaves. The chief end and object of life with the Kookie is, in fact, to kill his enemies, and there can be no greater virtue or glory than to do so. Diseases are believed to be inflicted by malevolent spirits who have to be pacified; and there is no other treatment for them. Some tribes burn their dead, along with different kinds of eatables given to the corpse; others bury them; but the burial day comes round once only in the year, and till its return each body is kept by in a shed, all the bodies being buried together when the day returns.

THE COSSYÁHS.

Adjoining the Kookies and the Meckirs are the Cossyáhs, usually called Khásiáhs in all the later official reports and other documents relating to them, but whom we prefer to call by their old name, if only to distinguish them from the Khásiáhs of Kumáon and Gurhwál. They are an athletic race of mountaineers, who are reputed to have frequently laid the plains of Assam under contribution in former times; but they are very well behaved at present, though still fond of martial exercises, and may be said to have become partially civilised as compared with the races by whom they are surrounded. The men have no hair on their face beyond a miserable wiry moustache, but make a good appearance notwithstanding; and the women are decidedly handsome, though not very cleanly. What is yet more remarkable of the race is that they are full of life and spirits, and are always singing, screaming, whistling, and running about, having great powers of industry though they are capricious in exerting them. The dress of the men consists of a *dhoti* and a long shirt without sleeves, over which a *chddur* is also occasionally worn; while the women wear a shapeless mantle of striped cotton cloth tied into a knot across the breast. The martial dress of the men substitutes a sleeveless tunic of long cloth for the shirt, the arms carried being a shield of buffalo hide or brass, a powerful two-handed sword, the bow and arrows, and a javelin. The use of poisoned arrows against wild beasts is common; but it speaks much for the manhood of ·the race that they have never been known to use them against their fellow creatures. Their common food comprises rice, millet, maize, *kochu*, and arrowroot, all of which are raised by themselves; besides which they also eat flesh of all kinds, including that of the leopard, and are especially fond of pork and dried fish. They do not drink milk, nor make any use of *ghee*, and are not partial to intoxicating liquors; but they are excessively fond of *páu*, a large supply of which they carry about with them and chew incessantly. This dyes their teeth and lips red, and they pride themselves on the dirty habit by saying that "dogs and Bengalis only have white teeth." Their progress in the industrial arts has not been very great, and being unacquainted with weaving they are obliged to get their clothes from other tribes.

The tribal divisions of the race are many, but they all combine to form a confederacy which, though not subject to a common superior, is yet amenable in some degree to the control of each clan. Their domestic relations are in several respects very peculiar. The husband does not take his wife home, but goes over to live with her at her father's house, almost like a retainer in her service. At one

time polyandry was very prevalent among them, but
that has now been supplanted by a great facility
of divorce. The marriage tie is so loose that
separation is signified simply by the exchange of
five cowries, and is constant, the children in every
case abiding with the mother. The law of inheritance
is equally curious, sister's children being recognised
by it as heirs in preference to one's own sons. The
religion of the race acknowledges the existence
of a Supreme Being, but more reverence is paid
by them to the inferior spirits believed to reside
in their hills and groves. They have great faith
also in omens, their divination being drawn principally from the breaking of eggs. Over the dead
there is a carousal continued for several days, in
which feasts, dances, mock fights, and fairs figure
prominently, a furious howling being also kept on.
The dead are burnt, but not necessarily at the
time of death, being often preserved a long time
for a more convenient season for disposing of
them. There are some monolithic monuments in
their hills, such as are also found in various
parts of Europe and Western Asia, consisting
of large flat circular slabs to sit upon, and also
of long upright pillars of irregular shape. These
are believed to be monuments raised over the
dead ; but it has not been ascertained by whom
and under what circumstances they were raised.

THE GÁROS.

To the west of the Cossyáhs are the Gáros, who inhabit the range of hills which divide Assam from Bengal Proper. This tract has been under British domination from 1822, but till recently the control of the Government extended only over the zemindáry and tributary Gáros, not over the independent clans who occupy the summits of the hills. The raids committed by these on their lowland neighbours were frequent, and this forced an expedition being undertaken against them in 1866, which finally resulted in the formation of the Gáro Hill district, which has been as successful as the similar arrangements in other places.

The older writers speak of the Gáros and Cossyáhs as one people; but this they are not, though there is certainly much similarity between them. The Gáros are of shorter make and harsher features than the Cossyáhs; but they are stout limbed and of great bodily strength like them, and a Gáro woman will carry over the hills a load which a Bengal cooly will with difficulty carry across the plains. The southern Gáros have the advantage of being stouter and better formed than their northern neighbours; but they are all equally ugly, and even their women are unlovely, though the girls are good humoured and have very musical voices. The temperament of the race is well spoken of. They are lively, goodnatured, hospitable, frank and honest, and very truthful. They are also affectionate fathers and kind husbands, and their respect for their women is evinced by all property-right being conceded to them. Among the evil customs prevalent amidst them, the immolation of human victims (who were always Bengalis) in honour of the dead was at one time very common; and they are still stanch slaveholders on a large scale, about two-fifths of the entire population of the country being dependent on the remaining three-fifths. The slaves are called *Nakal*, and the free men *Nákobá;* and the distinction between them is jealously preserved, though otherwise the slaves are not ill-treated, being well fed and well cared for, while they in return are devoted to their masters. The dress of the Gáros is very scanty. The males live almost wholly nude, their sole garment being a narrow strip of cloth worn as a girdle round the waist, which is passed from behind through the legs and brought up in the front. The female dress is nearly the same, consisting of a piece of cloth less than a foot in breadth wound round the loins, while all the other parts of the body are left bare. The ornaments worn by the women are earrings and bead necklaces; while many go altogether unadorned, accepting the verdict of the poet that beauty when unadorned is adorned the most. They eat all kinds of food, including cats, dogs, frogs, and snakes; and rear kine, goats, swine, fowls, and ducks. Like the

Nágás, Cossyáhs, and others, they abhor milk, and call it diseased matter. It is said that they are particularly fond of eating puppies, which they dress in a manner peculiar to themselves. The animal is fed with as large a quantity of rice as it will take, and is then roasted alive. When the roast is done, the puppy is cut up and eaten, the rice in its stomach being regarded as a delicacy. Their passion for drink is so great that liquor is given even to infants to swallow; and their excess in the indulgence is often productive of bloody brawls, which are more frequent, however, among the southern than among the northern Gáros, the latter being provoked by drink only to more dancing and music.

The houses of the Gáros are called *changs*, and are from thirty to one-hundred-and-fifty feet in length, and from ten to forty in breadth. They are roofed with thatch, or with mats of long grass, and propped up with *sál* timbers, of which the beams also are made. The sides are constructed of hollow bamboos cut open and woven like a mat. Every house is divided into two parts, the upper and the lower, the latter being allotted to cattle and poultry. The upper story is subdivided into distinct enclosures for the owner and his wife and their unmarried daughters and other children generally, while the unmarried sons are housed separately in a bachelors' hall, with which every village is provided. The total number of houses in a village is about twenty,

o

and they are almost all of them substantially built.
One peculiarity to be noted is that the villages or
clans are divided into *Máháris*, or "motherhoods,"
particular Máháris being especially connected with
and intermarrying into each other. A man's sister
marries in the family from which he derives his
wife; his son may marry a daughter of that sister,
and, as male heirs do not inherit, the son-in-law,
succeeding his father-in-law in right of his wife, gets
his father's sister, who is his wife's mother, as an
additional wife to live with. The marriage process
is also peculiar. The selection is made by the girl,
and the male can make no advances till the female's
wishes are known. The consent of the parents of
the parties is implied, with this proviso—that, if the
old people refuse, they can be beaten into compliance.
After these preliminaries have been settled, the female
and her party again take the initiative and proceed
to the house of the bridegroom to secure him, while
he pretends to run away from them. He is quickly
caught, and, in spite of resistance offered, is married,
amidst lamentations and counterfeit grief both on his
part and on the part of his parents. The ceremony
is completed by the sacrifice of a cock and a hen,
when the piteous howls of the bridegroom and his
party subside under the usual debaucheries of a
feast. Her husband thus secured, the wife usually
becomes a good helpmate to him, sharing in all
the labours of husbandry, besides being his guardian

angel at home. One couple usually cultivates from three to four *beegáhs* of land a year, and three crops are raised on it in rotation, namely, the *dousáhán*, cotton, and millet. The chief productions of the Gáro hills are: cotton, *dousáhán*, maize, millet, chillies, and yams. It is on cotton chiefly that the people depend for those necessaries of life which their hills will not yield. They are, besides, good workers in iron and bell-metal, and make *koráhs* or *tháHees* of the latter which are much prized in Bengal. Their implements of husbandry are: a hoe, a *dáo*, and a battle-axe, which is used for all purposes. No Gáro is ever seen without the axe, except when a spear is substituted for it to answer any especial purpose. The wilder Gáros protect their villages in war time by stockading them, and by blocking up all approaches to them with felled trees, besides which *pánjees*, or sharp bamboo spikes, are thickly planted, and so deep that they cannot be extracted, the only way to remove them being to shave them even with the ground. The religion of the people recognises a great god named Kishijee, the character given to whom is very like that of the Hindu god Siva; but they make no images of him, and have no temples to worship him in. What they are commonly seen to adore is the bamboo adorned with flowers and tufts of cotton thread. They burn their dead, and bury the ashes exactly where the pile was kindled, over which a hut is often erected in which the wearing apparel of the deceased is deposited.

CHAPTER IV.

TRIBES ON THE EASTERN FRONTIER.

THE chief tribes on the eastern frontier are the Kookies, to whom we have already referred, the Joomeáhs or Mughs, the Kheongthás, who are so like the Joomeáhs in all respects as to require no separate notice, and the Shindoos; and, lower down, the Khoomeás, the Koos, the Mroos or Mroo Khyens, and the Khyens. All the races are extremely migratory. They occupy small hamlets surrounded by bamboo stockades perched on the top of almost inaccessible hills ; but where one sees a village at one time he finds nothing but a jungle six months after, the people inhabiting the village having moved off perhaps to half a day's, or a whole day's journey thence, transporting the very name of the village with their huts. In character some of the tribes are exceedingly inoffensive, while others are the very reverse of it, of which latter description are the Lusháis, Shindoos, and Koos, who are only known for their plundering expeditions and the outrages they perpetrate.

THE JOOMEÁHS.

The Joomeáhs, or Mughs, are understood to be the aboriginal inhabitants of Arracan, but now occupy in great numbers the hill-tracts of Chittagong, or rather that portion of them which is known by the name of the *Kápás Mahal*, or the cotton districts. They are called *Joomeáhs* because they cultivate by burning, the word *joom* in their language meaning "to burn." The plough is never used by them, and, in fact, they never cultivate land even enough for a plough to operate upon. They cut the jungle on their hill-sides and then set fire to it, the ashes being spread over and dug into the ground to manure it, after which the seeds are sown in the same manner as by other wild tribes generally. The personal appearance of the race is very like that of the Chinese, and especially distinguished by high and broad cheek bones, flat noses, and oblique eyes. Their forms are short, but well made and athletic, and their colour is of the mulatto kind. The hair of both sexes is glossy and black, and they are equally proud of its quality. The women wear it parted in the middle and tied in a knot at the back of the head; while the men put on a kind of turban of white cloth, which is entwined with their hair. The dress of the women consists of a cloth tightly bound round the bosom and flowing to the feet, with a large outer covering thrown over the whole person reaching to the knees; while that of the men is composed of one cloth wound round the middle and another thrown over the shoulders. The only ornaments worn by the women are thick earrings of various designs, to make room for which the lobes of their ears are widely perforated, those of the men being similarly bored to put in their cigars. The huts of the race are made of bamboos raised on piles several feet above the ground; each house being occupied by one family only, excluding the bachelors, who have a common dwelling allowed to them in every village. Their ordinary food is boiled rice and fish; but animals are also eaten, and nothing from the smallest to the biggest is indifferent to them. Both sexes smoke and chew tobacco; and they are also fond of *páu*, but do not drink much habitually. They are reputed to be very long-lived, and retain their strength and faculties to a great age; and altogether they are much less wild than the races by whom they are surrounded. The rich among them burn, while the poor bury, their dead, and with both a funeral is the occasion of mirth and rejoicing, which frequently end in dissipation and excess.

THE SHINDOOS.

The Shindoos occupy the forest tract between the valley of the Irráwádi and Arracan, to the east of the boundary range, the Lusháí Kookies residing on its west. Numerically they are less strong than several races living near them, notably than the Khoomeás; but they are held in greater dread all over the frontier, even the Khoomeás being afraid of them. Their raids into Chittagong were at one time very frequent, the chief object always held in view by them being the capture of slaves. The villages proceeded against were invariably attacked at night and set on fire, and of those of the inhabitants who could not escape the males were killed and the females and children were carried off. These outrages have now been greatly checked ; but the character of the race has not yet very materially improved. Their houses are built on raised platforms and are generally well made, bamboos or timber being used in their construction according to the wealth of the owners, and the thatching being of grass. They cultivate also with industry, and raise all the grains usually grown in jungly hills, such as maize, *basrá*, hill-rice, yams, *kudoos*, ginger, *til*, linseed, cotton, and sugar-cane. They are rich too in pigs and poultry, but are more fond of dogs as food, and eat all sorts of game, including elephants. The arms used by the warriors are bows and arrows, short spears, and shields made of buffalo-hide. Muskets are also prized, and many have been secured and are often very mischievously used, the position occupied by them being too remote for any very effective control

being exercised over them. Wives amongst them
are always purchased, and polygamy is widely
prevalent, almost every man having from two to
four wives. Their religion is Buddhism, but so
corrupted as to be hardly recognisable. The dead
are buried by them in a supine posture, with the
head to the east; and with the warrior are buried
his weapons and his gongs.

THE KIIOOMEÁS.

The Khoomeás occupy the country on both banks
of the Koladyne river, from Thánnáh Koladyne to
the mouth of the Sullá Kheong, and form the largest
and most important of all the wild tribes in that
direction. They are divided into many classes, of
whom the most powerful are the Khoongchoo,
Khoong, Ánoo, and Yeasing. The primary occupation of all of them is agriculture; besides which they
also manufacture cloths, spears, and gunpowder; and
all, or nearly all of them, practise dacoity. Their
principal arm is the musket: but spears and shields
are also used. Each tribe has its own chief, the
confederate chiefs together representing the sovereign
power.

THE KOOS.

The Koos inhabit the mountainous regions near
the sources of the Lemroo and its principal feeder

the Peng Kheong. They are near neighbours to the
Khoomeás, and differ little from them in habits, but
exceed them, in barbarity. They are extremely wild,
and are always at feud, either among themselves or
with the other tribes about them. They have little
or no clothing, but canes slit up in two and painted
red are wrapped round the stomach as a protection in
war. Their arms are the musket, the spear, and the
bow and arrows. One striking peculiarity to be noted
of them is that they drink the blood of animals ; and
a well approved custom with them on festive occasions
is to tie a bull or *gyál* (wild ox) to a stake, and to
pierce him with spears, after which bamboo cups are
applied to the wounds, from which men, women, and
children drink the warm blood with great gusto.

THE MROOS.

The Mroos occupy the country north of the junction
of the Saeng Kheong with the Lemroo. They are a
quiet and inoffensive race, largely given to cultivation.
The males frequently go naked, or have only a rag
fastened in front below the loins, except in the cold
weather when a cloak also is occasionally thrown
over the body. The dress of the females is a dark
blue cotton gown fastened at the neck and descend-
ing to the knees. Persons labouring under palsy,
ulcers, leprosy, and other incurable diseases, are
viewed by them as outcasts, and are not permitted to

reside in the same place with the rest, a separate
village being assigned to them, in which, however,
they are well cared for and supported.

THE KIIYENS.

The last tribe we shall notice are the Khyens,
who inhabit the mountains between Arracan and
Ává. They are very dissimilar to the Mughs, but
resemble the Mroos so much that the two have
been held by several writers to be only different
tribes of the same race, which is highly probable.
The Khyens live for the most part in the thickest
retreats of their forests, and, being erratic in their
habits, are constantly going about in parties, and
pitch their tents wherever they can find fertile spots
to cultivate. Their devotion to cultivation is greater
even than that of the Mroos, and they raise large
supplies of rice and vegetables, which form their
staple food. They also eat fish and the flesh of
any animal they can procure, except of the tiger,
bear, and otter; and their time is mainly taken
up with hunting, fishing, and agriculture. They
moreover collect iron-ore, honey, and elephants'
tusks, which they sell and barter for such luxuries
as they cannot produce themselves. The principal
occupations of their women are spinning, weaving,
and cookery, besides which they also assist the
men in their field labours. What they are, however,

most remarkable for is the custom of tattooing
their faces, which makes them hideous, though the
marks and figures drawn are in themselves often
very artistic and curious. The origin of the practice
is thus accounted for:—They say that the Tártárs
in the days of their power imposed upon all their
subject races the payment of a tribute in women,
whereupon the Khyen ladies decided on sacrificing
their charms so as to make the tribute from their
tribe unacceptable. The plan must have been
eminently successful; it is certain that the custom
of tattooing is now on the decline. The dress of
the women consists of a black petticoat reaching
to the knee, with a looser garment over it, while
that of the men comprises a piece of blue cloth
wound round the loins with one end of it dangling
before, and the other dangling behind, and a cloth
wound round the head, a jacket being also worn
by those who can afford to have one. The arms
of the men are the spear, and crossbow and arrows;
but they are used only against wild beasts, the
Khyens having no other enemies to fight with.
Their villages consist usually of from fifteen to
twenty houses each, over which there is a headman
called *Táyi* or *Nandáyi*. Each house has ordinarily
two apartments only, one for sleeping and the
other for cooking in; and underneath the floor are
lodged their swine and poultry. On getting married
the Khyen always goes to live with his wife at

her father's house, and never brings her thence till
after the birth of one or two children. No dowry
is given at marriage, and the union is dissoluble ·
at the will of the parties, at a moment's warning,
without any reason being required to be assigned
for the severance. There are feasts given on occasions of both marriages and deaths, the choicest
delicacies indulged in being pork and rice-beer.
The religion of the race is confined to the propitiation of spirits, to whom sacrifices are made.
The dead are burnt, and their bones buried in
some distant mountain.

PART III.

GENERAL REMARKS.

THE stages of wild life are the savage and hunter state, the nomadic or herdsman state, and the agricultural state; of which the first appears to have long been passed by most of the tribes to whom we have referred, for, though hunting be still an occupation well prized by many of them, there is not one that lives by it exclusively at this day. Even the second stage has been passed by several tribes, though by far the greater number of them have only partially abandoned it, living as nomadic-cultivators, which is a compound of the second and third stages, and in different grades of advancement in that state. Under a well-ordered Government, the nomadic state is of course being rapidly changed for the agricultural one; but up to this time there are more nomadic cultivators among the wild tribes than regular tillers of the soil. The mode of cultivation followed is, we have seen, exceedingly simple and primitive, and almost identical in all places, though the races practising it are widely separated from, and have almost no sort of connexion with, each other. It has different names in different places, being called *dhdi-yd* in the Central Provinces, *jooming* in the Hill Tracts of Chittagong, *toung-yd* in Arracan, etc.; but the process followed, which we have described, is in every case the same. All the tribes are given to living on the skirts of forests, mainly for the facility it gives them to effect clearances in the manner to which they are so partial. Few of them cultivate the same field more than two or three years, by which time the soil is held to have become perfectly exhausted, when they move on to new unbroken forests, never thinking of returning to the old ones till they have relapsed to their original jungly state. As there is abundance of virgin soil around them, they are thus constantly moving about by choice; and the herdsman's life which they also follow offers no hindrance to this, since they always carry their flocks and herds with them, it being, in fact, imperative on them to do so, owing to the general scantiness of the food-grains raised by them. The wildernesses roamed through also abound with game of all kinds, such as the bison, the buffalo, the elk, the wild hog, and the hare, and these form additional food articles for them, which makes them almost independent of their crops in unfavourable seasons. The jungles abound, moreover, with tigers, hyænas, and wolves; and it is a matter of necessity to the tribes living with them to acquire the art of killing them, and hence the prolonged indulgence of the hunting propensity in them even after the first stage of savage existence has been passed. It is this inclination of theirs, allied with their isolation, that seems to have taught them the more reprehensible use of their arms for which most of them were long so particularly famous. The roads from district to district necessarily passed over their hills and through their jungles, and this gave them the opportunity to levy tolls and blackmail from the traders and wayfarers who frequented them, which soon degenerated into open pillage and wholesale robbery, too often accompanied by the sacrifice of human lives.

Living in this manner, almost all the wild tribes have always remained confined within the nooks and corners into which they were forced when the immigrant races became a collected people, and have been necessarily far removed from the pale of civilisation. Of themselves, they have never sought, even in settled times, to cultivate the acquaintance of their neighbours, preferring to remain in barbarism in the hiding-places selected by their ancestors, and apparently thriving best in localities where no other human being could have existed. Those who live in forests say that they cannot endure the climate of the plains, where the heat gives them fever; those who inhabit the Terái, such as the Meches, have never attempted to get into higher ranges, which they assert do not agree with them; and

those living inland, such as the Gonds, find that
the sea air is fatal to them. So unhealthy are the
places they occupy, that even those people of the
plains who are in the habit of periodically visiting
them—such as elephant-hunters, corn-dealers, money-
lenders, and the collectors of jungle produce—seldom
return from their annual expeditions without suffering
in health, and yet none of the wild tribes betray any
trace of sickliness about them, exhibiting, on the contrary, the most wonderful immunity from the effects
of the malaria in which they live imbedded. This
may, perhaps, be accepted as a proof of the antiquity
of the races concerned, for they must have occupied
their present corners for many centuries to have
become so well acclimatised to them. The jungles
are thinly populated, and, as a rule, the wild tribes
procreate scantily, which accounts for their not being
seen to increase in numbers in any place; and in
particular localities they have further done all in
their power to limit population by the adoption
of such institutions as polyandry and infanticide.
But they are hale and hearty-looking everywhere,
much more so, certainly, than the natives of the
plains, who are increasing in numbers at a rate
that threatens to be perplexing to the politicians
and administrators of a future day; and the only
explanation the result admits of is, that they have
got quite accustomed to live and thrive on the
noxious exhalations they inhale.

The oldest Hindu books, again, speak of the *Dasyas* as a black race, and most of the internal tribes we have described are found to be very much darker than the Hindus and Mahomedans by whom they are surrounded, which may be accepted as another proof of their antiquity, since they must have occupied their present habitations in their distinctness from time anterior to or coeval with the establishment of the Hindu and Mahomedan races around them, and refused ever after to intermix with them. They have lived almost wholly by themselves, and where they have done so have retained their original colour undiluted, and not their colour only, but all the other peculiarities by which they were distinguished from the commencement. Almost all these races have less height, less symmetry, and more dumpiness and flesh than the peoples surrounding them ; broader and flatter faces, shorter and wider noses, smaller eyes, larger ears, thicker lips, and deficient beards. In their eagerness to be considered respectable they often pretend to a descent from the Rájpoots ; but the proofs patent in their features are unmistakable, and proclaim them to be of much older date than the Rájpoots, or their ancestors the Kshetriyas, can count in India. In the case of the frontier tribes their resemblance in features to the races living beyond them is easily traced ; all the tribes on the western frontier having the Afghán or Beloochee appearance stamped on

P

them ; all those on the northern frontier bearing as
deeply indented marks of a Thibetan origin ; all
those on the eastern frontier, of Burmese extraction ;
and all those on the north-eastern frontier exhibiting
a compound of the Burman and Chinese features
blended in varied shades. This proves the tribes
to be either half-breeds or immigrants of old date
long settled in the districts they now inhabit. But
the features of the internal tribes are, like their
colour, not traceable to any of the races surrounding
them, and this distinctiveness they undoubtedly owe
to the utter isolation in which they have always lived
in their present quarters from the earliest times. Till
recently they had no contact of any sort with aliens
and strangers on any pretence whatever. The
conveniences of life, where they had them, were
such only as could be secured by self-labour, even
the manufactures and arts being mostly domestic.
Almost everywhere every man made his own house,
conducted his own agriculture, and brewed his own
beer, all which is done in most places in the same
way even now. Smiths, carpenters, potters, and
weavers did not exist before among them, and
where existing at present are mostly foreigners
recently admitted, and are barely allowed to live
within hailing distance, not being suffered to intermix
with them. It is not likely, therefore, that the
dissimilarity so peculiar to the different tribes will
be early effaced.

The blessings of civilisation among most of the tribes are now mainly represented by the presence of the *mahájuns*, money-lenders, and spirit-sellers, who have forced themselves into their company simultaneously with the artisan classes, in comparatively modern times. Their contact with these is generally held to have deteriorated their character; but this conclusion does not seem to be absolutely correct. If the intercourse has deteriorated their character to any extent in particular respects, it has certainly improved it in others in a greater degree; and their only hope of civilisation rests on such communion becoming closer day by day. What the Government has done amongst them is mainly confined to the putting down of the depredations and outrages which used to be so frequently committed by them, and this has been effected either by the strong hand of power, or by conciliation, or by compounding with their supposed rights to levy tolls or to pillage by paying regular stipends to them. Thus quieted, peaceful occupations have also commenced to be taught to them, which has induced habitual raiders and caterans to settle down as cultivators, and to colonise their own hill sides. But there was a mediatory go-between class wanted to humanise them, and, as none others cared to approach them, there was no option but to depend on the *mahájuns*, money-lenders, and spirit-sellers for exerting their kind offices in this way, to which they have done as much justice as could have been expected from them. The Gonds are said to have been at one time in the habit of feasting on their sick relatives, and even now some small tribes in Amarkantak and Chatisgurh have the credit of doing so. If these practices have declined in the greater part of their country at the present day, as they have undoubtedly done, that is solely attributable to the good offices of such intervening classes as the Brinjáris.

Nothing tends so much to confusion as excessive generalisations, and the good faith and manly character evidently belonging to some tribes have been very wrongly understood to be common to many of them. The truthfulness and honesty of some of the races are certainly remarkable, at least in their dealings with each other. Their right to the soil appropriated by them they consider to be unquestionable. "I am the proprietor of the land" is the boast alike of the Bheel, the Gond, the Meená, and the Sonthál. But this is only an assertion of right as against the Sovereign and the zemindár; no conflict arises among themselves on this account. When one person has commenced operations on a particular spot, no other man ever comes forward to claim it. When crops are raised they are cut and gathered without any contention. In several places even the granaries are left unprotected and unsecured, as no one ever thinks of appropriating what does not belong to himself. And the flocks and herds of different owners constantly

run into each other without causing much quarrel or
ill-feeling between them. These, however, are the
usual Arcadian traits of savage life all over the
world, and the same man who will not harbour
a thought of over-reaching or robbing his brother
savage unhesitatingly waylays, robs, and even
murders without compunction the unwary traveller
crossing his path. Here it is not so much an
abstract question of honesty or dishonesty, as of the
form in which they are severally exhibited. The
descriptions which represent the wild tribes as being
simple-hearted, good-natured, and inoffensive, are
true in their integrity only of such inland tribes as
the Sonthåls, Koles, and Bhooyåns, and of such
borderers as the Khåsiåhs of Gurhwål and Kumåon,
but not of the rest. Many of the tribes have been
lauded, and justly, for their love of truth and high-
mindedness; but these are common traits with men
who have always lived free. A rude respect for
women has also been counted as the distinguishing
virtue of some tribes; but that respect seems often to
be qualified in several places to a considerable extent.
The Khonds admit women into their general councils,
but bring forward no subjects before them which
have not been previously sat upon. The Meekirs
eat tiger's flesh, but withhold it from their females
lest it should make them too strong-minded for
control. The Boksås do not allow their women to
drink spirits, on the plea that their condition and

duties do not require the use of stimulants. Among
most of the tribes, moreover, the hardest drudgeries
of life are always imposed on the women, and the
show of respect towards them virtually resolves itself
only to a concession made for reconciling them to
their lot. A few tribes excepted, almost all the
others have always had the credit of great agility
and bravery, which combined to make them the
good caterans in their native fastnesses which till
recently they were. This pluckiness is, in the eyes
of Englishmen, their highest virtue, and advantage
has already been taken to convert those into soldiers
whom it was possible to trust with arms and accoutre-
ments. There are Bheel, Mair, and Kookie corps in
the Indian service at this moment; the Bhaugulpore
Hill Rangers, when they existed, were composed of
Páháriáhs; and the police battalions all over the
country include a large number of local wild men
in their ranks. But with this pluckiness were allied
a multitude of sins which it was not possible for it
either to cover or palliate. All these spirited tribes
are likewise spoken of as being hospitable, and some
of them as being even social. But their hospitality
and sociality have invariably been represented by a
continued round of festivities and debaucheries, from
one end of the year to the other, which has contributed more perhaps than anything else to their
degradation. That examples so bright might
never be lost sight of, it is the practice, we have

seen, with some tribes to hang up the skulls of the animals killed and eaten in the halls of the entertainers, as records of their worth and for inciting their children to follow in their footsteps. After this, it is scarcely right to attribute any degeneracy in their character to their dealings with the *mahájuns* and money-lenders, or even to their connexion with the spirit-sellers. Of course the spirit-seller does a great deal of mischief wherever he goes; but the appetite he goes to feed existed in all the wilds and mountain fastnesses of India long before he approached them. Among several races we see private morals so carefully watched over that the unmarried youths of both sexes are kept apart at night, not only from each other, but even from the married members of their own families, lest there should be any lapse of virtue within the family circle itself; but we read in the same breath of such beastly customs as the *Bandana* among the Sonthals, and the promiscuous intercourse of the sexes in various other shapes among many of the other tribes; of the wide prevalence of polygamy and polyandry; and of marriages taking place on credit, and the free exchange and divorce of wives. Among the Bheels, Mairs, Khonds, and others, a man takes a wife and keeps her so long as he likes her, but when they get tired of each other he transfers her, or she transfers herself, over to a third person without hesitation; and among

the Kookies all the women of a village, married or
unmarried, are at all times available to the chief at
his will. In communities where such practices have
long been in existence, even the spirit-seller had
hardly any greater enormity to introduce.

Few of the wild tribes have any religion of their
own, or any adequate idea of God, though they all,
more or less, admit His existence, and even the
existence of the soul and of futurity. All their
notions on these subjects are, in fact, seemingly
borrowed from among the superstitions of their
neighbours; and in this way Hinduism has been
acting with much force on them, and is fast drawing
them down into its own vortex, which may in the
future give them a civilisation such as it is not in the
power of the Government to confer. Most of the
divinities set up at present are the ogres of Hindu
mythology, and the worship everywhere, except
among the Himálayan tribes, is devil-worship *par
excellence*, which was always attended in the past—
that is, so long as it was possible for it to be
so attended—with human sacrifices. But this state
of things must mend when the adoption of Hinduism
is complete and its better features are appreciated.
The rites which have been most widely accepted up
to this time are those observed on occasions of births,
marriages, and deaths, all of which are followed
with much fidelity; and there is certainly nothing
particularly revolting in them. As a rule the wild

tribes are even more superstitious than the Hindus; but they have this advantage over them, that they are not priest-ridden to the same or to any great extent. The Bráhman was an object of hatred to all of them, and they allow no interference on the part of their priest (the substitute of the Bráhman among them) with their domestic duties and affairs. Where any interference in such matters is called for, it comes from the elders of the people chosen by themselves, or from their chiefs, the priest's duties being confined to the celebration of the festivals; and this is an enormous advantage, the effects of which ought to be very salutary.

General Briggs, in his *Lecture on the Wild Tribes,* sums up the differences between them and the Hindus to the following effect:—(1) The Hindus are divided into castes; the aborigines have no such distinctions: (2) The Hindu widows do not remarry; the widows of the aborigines do, mostly taking the younger brothers of their former husbands: (3) The Hindus venerate the cow and abstain from beef; the aborigines feed on all flesh alike: (4) The Hindus abstain from drinks; the aborigines delight in them, and even their religious ceremonies are not complete without them: (5) The Hindus prepare their own food, or take only what has been prepared by a higher caste; the aborigines partake of food prepared by any one: (6) The Hindus do not shed blood habitually; but no ceremony of the aborigines is

complete without the shedding of blood : (7) The
Hindus have a caste of priests ; the aborigines select
their priests out of those particularly skilled in
magic, or sorcery, or divination, or in curing diseases,
etc.: (8) The Hindus burn their dead ; the aborigines
mostly bury them : (9) The Hindu civil institutions
are municipal; those of the aborigines are patriarchal :
(10) And, lastly', the Hindus have known letters and
sciences and the art of writing for more than three
thousand years; while the aborigines are, now at
least, illiterate. This comparison does not show that
the aborigines were in many respects open to further
deterioration of character by coming into contact
with the Hindus. The Hindus are a cleanly people,
while the aborigines are excessively dirty, and are
now only barely learning the use of water from their
neighbours. Some of the frontier tribes, who are not
aborigines, are certainly better housed, better fed, and
better clothed than those of the plains; but this,
which reads as an anomaly, is easily accounted for.
Their food is more easily got, and, as they have no
prejudices of caste, they do not stick at anything,
several tribes not objecting to feed even on tigers,
rhinoceroses, dogs, and vermin of all kinds, which
always gives them variety and abundance, if not
provisions of the choicest kinds. Their clothing is
more difficult to get at ; but, being absolutely
necessary, owing to the climate of their hills and
forests, has to be got, and is got, mostly from the

civilised races living beyond their limits. Their
houses, for the same reason, have to be better and
more strongly built, and, the materials for them being
easily available in their forests, it was not difficult
to learn the art of so constructing them. These
advantages apart, they have none over the people
of the plains; and, if they are ever humanised to
any appreciable extent, it must be by imitating
them.

INDEX.

	PAGE		PAGE
Ábors	154	Bnars	90
Bomjoer	,,	Bhátoos	21
Bor	,,	Bheels	23
Membu	,,	Bartí	32
Fádoo	22	Burdá	17
Púshee	22	Dáungchee	31
Silook	10	Doreyle	32
Sissee	17	Kárit	16
Áfreedees	122	Khoteel	31
Ádum	123	Kotwál	32
Ákú	,,	Mowchee	22
Bhyrám	,,	Mutwáreo	,,
Karum	22	Nohál	31
Meerie	12	Nalkrá	32
Ooláh	10	Nirdhi	31
Orukrye	16	Pággi	32
Ákhús	149	Parvee	,,
Házíri-Khiwá	150	Powerd	,,
Káppáchore	,,	Turree	31
Baloochees	117	Wulvee	32
Boogti	118	Wurálá	16
Bozdár	42	Wusáwú	,,
Ghoorcháni	12	Bhooyáns	60
Khutrúni	12	Bhotees	127
Koráh	22	Bhowris	29
Kasráni	12	Bokaás	130
Lishári	,,	Mehrús	132
Mádári	,,	Booteáhs	140
Singhárl	,,	Dharmáus	141

	PAGE
Brinjáris	16
Bunnoochees	121
Cáchicete	175
Hazú	176
Purbutteáh	,,
Seroniáh	,,
Shargiah	,,
Cheroos	90
Cossyáhs	188
Dháttis	55
Dhimáls	143
Duflás	150
Eriligáru	112
Gárus	191
Gipsies	115
Gonds	1
Dádávie	9
Dholi	,,
Coor	,,
Gurráh	5
Jártiá	,,
Kátulyá	9
Khullottee	5
Kolkopál	9
Kolkábhutu;	,,
Kolám	,,
Koorkee	5
Mánjee	,,
Máree	,,
Madyál	9
Ojhyál	11
Pádal	,,
Ráj	5
Rughuwál	9
Thotyál	,,
Grásiás	42
Jháreja	43
Wagelá	,,
Introductory Remarks	ix
Joomeáhs	197

	PAGE
Kanjhars	90
Kaorwás	55
Kárubárus	113
Kárwárs	90
Bhográh	91
Khurriáh	,,
Kattis	43
Ehwarutlá	46
Khachur	,,
Khoomán	,,
Wálá	,,
Kattouries	47
Kerántis	135
Khámptis	163
Kháslahs	128
Kheongthás	196
Khonds	95
Benniáh	100
Bhetidh	,,
Málláh	,,
Khoomeás	200
Anoo	,,
Khoong	,,
Khapngchoo	,,
Yeaxing	,,
Khyens	202
Kochas	146
Rájbunsis	147
Kohátees	113
Kolarian and other races in Bengal, The	59
Koles	60
Bhoomíj	,,
Choodr	,,
Hos	,,
Larká	,,
Moondá	,,
Kolls	39
Ábeev	41
Bábriáh	42

	PAGE			PAGE
Kolis—			**Mishmees—**	
Dháuodhám	42		Myjoo	160
Dhour	41		Táen	,,
Doongury	,,		Tshee	,,
Kákret	42		Momunds	124
Mullár	41		Álumzye	,,
Murvee	42		Báoezye	,,
Pultunwirrii	,,		Khwázye	,,
Ráj	41		Michmee	,,
Solesy	,,		Pindee Áli	,,
Sone	42		Tourkzye	,,
Towkry	41		Mroos	201
Tulluhdáh	42		Mudikpors	22
Kookles	179		Mughs	197
Chuckmá	,,		Murmis	134
Lunctá	,,		Murwátees	122
Lushái	,,		Nágás	167
Reing	,,		Angámi	168
Rhangkol	181		Lotáh	,,
Tipperáh	179		Rengmá	,,
Koos	200		Náts	90
Koráwárs	21		Niadis	114
Kurumhárs	113		Oráons	78
Lepchás	137		Páháriáhs	83
Khambá	,,		Máls	85
Rong	,,		Malers	,,
Limboos	133		Kumárs	,,
Hung	134		Part I.—The Internal Tribes	1
Rái	,,		Part II.—The Frontier Tribes	117
Lobannás	56		Part III.—General Remarks	205
Mairs and Meenás	50		**Páthàns**	119
Meches	143		Bungáish	,,
Meekirs	178		Puttooás	92
Meerás	151		Rebáttis	56
Mishmees	159		Souriás	107
Choulkáttá	160		Sehriás	57
Dháh	,,		Chándlá	,,
Mannedh	,,		Kossál	,,
Mároo	,,		Sudání	,,
Mleo	,,		**Shindoos**	198

	PAGE
Singphos	165
Sodás	54
Soligás	113
Soathóls	69
Báskí	76
Besárá	,,
Chordi	,,
Hánadá	,,
Hemruo	,,
Kiskts	,,
Márlí	,,
Murmu	,,
Saran	,,
Tudi	,,
Sours	93
Swátees	125
Táreemooks	20
Thároos	132
Thotl	57
Todás	109
Kenná	110
Kattan	,,
Peikee	,,
Pekkan	,,

	PAGE
Todas—	
Tudi	110
Tribes in Western India	23
Tribes of the Central Provinces	1
Tribes of the Madrás Presidency	95
Tribes of Rájpootáná and the Indian Desert	50
Tribes on the Eastern Frontier	196
Tribes on the Northern Frontier	127
Tribes on the North-eastern Frontier	148
Tribes on the North-western Frontier	117
Váyus	135
Wussucrás	130
Áhmedzye	,,
Bithunnee	,,
Máhsud	,,
Othmánzye	,,

THE END.

THOS. DE LA RUE AND CO., PRINTERS, BUNHILL ROW, LONDON.

CPSIA information can be obtained
at www.ICGtesting.com
Printed in the USA
LVOW12s0525150917
548811LV00002B/420/P